STARS N GRIPES

STARS N GRIPES

From the Writings of Jonny Carter

A Novel

Jonny Carter

iUniverse, Inc.

New York Lincoln Shanghai

Stars n Gripes
From the Writings of Jonny Carter

iUniverse books may be ordered through booksellers or by contacting:

iUniverse
2021 Pine Lake Road, Suite 100
Lincoln, NE 68512
www.iuniverse.com
1-800-Authors (1-800-288-4677)

Because of the dynamic nature of the Internet, any Web addresses or links contained in this book may have changed since publication and may no longer be valid.

This is a work of fiction. All of the characters, names, incidents, organizations, and dialogue in this novel are either the products of the author's imagination or are used fictitiously.

Titled by Bounce.

Artwork by the Stu Francis Studio.

ISBN: 978-0-595-43462-6 (pbk)
ISBN: 978-0-595-87789-8 (ebk)

Printed in the United States of America

STARS N GRIPES

#1: Smoke the Whole Fucking Village

Big City British Boy Unpeels the Fuss about the Apple. Thoughts from a foreign seed.

So nice they named it twice—we'll see. As a more prudent man than I once blessed, "If the world had a capital, it would be New York." As a city inappropriate enough not to govern its own country, could New York possibly command a planet? With no other authority than my pen, I ramble around, hauling with me a mild alcoholic impediment, twenty cigarettes, my erudite wisdom, and a hometown reputation now vanished, only to be reinstate-sided.

By way of introduction: An eighteen-month contract coaching soccer skills to the affluent communities of rural Jersey bridged the North Atlantic and abandoned my cute butt and quaint accent to the States, verging on the city limits of the greatest metropolitan prospect ever to be conceived. Of Welsh descent, I have seen a few things and have been a few things, though I'm definitely no concession to the truth. I just choose to write my opinion. With any personal responsibility jettisoned the second that my passport was stamped, I let myself be limitless to roam. Buoyed by the potential and the sanguinity of the restricted metropolis, I scampered with fistfuls of dollars and with the heart of an endeavourer towards the insomnious city.

The Lincoln Tunnel, a tube far too long to hold your breath all the way through, revealed to me the false heart of the city: Times Square. Flashing lights, shiny lights, and Japanese. You never get a second chance to make a first impression, and I can't say that I was best pleased straight off the bat. Foul ball. We don't belong here, and so I flippantly toss my all-enlightening map that delivered little towards a garbage can. It rims the can and falls to the ground. I pick it up. Littering charges would be an unnecessary beginning. Unguided, I decide to pursue the unmistakable pheromone of instinct. Striding mile after mile of avenue and farther of cross street, turning left if to my right offered a sightseeing zeitgeist of the city tour guide—the picture-postcard New York I can leave to picture postcards. The *streets* condone realism and sincere reflection, so there, my friend, we will stay. Though how do you judge a town? There is of course only one true appraisal of a city's meaning and worth, and for those of us lucky enough to properly understand the regime of drinking, the evidence of merit that is to be arbitrated is that of the supply chain of alcohol.

The search is on. We know exactly what we are looking for—let's go and find it. To my incredulity, every bar in New York is of Irish extraction. Every bar. You do know that the Irish are not the only race to manufacture, retail, or consume beer. A whole bunch of other countries now fabricate and devour bucket loads of beverage. A veritable wide variety of alcoholic options are available to the liquid shopper. But my virgin tourist perception is that the New Yorker wants his bar verified with Irish validation, bejewelled with a ceiling adorned rusty bicycle, Guinness memorabilia, and farming utensils that may have once occupied native hands that facilitated the liberation of potatoes from the earth. They also may not have, though. They could perhaps just have been purchased in a job lot from an Irish bar wholesaler working out of a shady part of town—McCormack Bar Parts of Brooklyn. I don't know. Is this what you want? Because this is what you have. Whereas familiarity procreates security, and you should stick with what you know, fix nothing that isn't broken, and never diversify too far from your core competency. But what the fuck? You could mix up your bar scene a little. Remember the childhood enjoyment of a Christmas selection box—selection being the operative word here.

The concept of the Irish American as a demographic is of considerable intrigue for me. Correct me if I am wrong, and I'm sure that you will exercise this most American of traits, but every New Yorker seems to want to be an Irish American ... but then there are a few who want to be Italian American ... and a few who want to be African American. Nobody here wants to be just *American*.

After two hundred and something years of independence, we can't still be on the first generation of migrants, can we?

Surely an origin gets diluted until your origin is where you are. The family of Uncle Paulie, who was born in Palermo, Sicily, and immigrated to New York at the age of twenty-one in 1922, is Italian American and justifiably so. Cousin Tito, born in Newark during the mid-eighties, is not Italian American, but just American. Is that not how it works? Why can't you guys be just American? Why do you need to hang on to some heritage that just isn't *your* heritage? This apparent contradiction appears ubiquitous amongst all the New Yorkers that I have met—the contradiction being that you are undoubtedly one of the most patriotic countries, which is to your credit, yet some why you hold this enigmatic lingering union to your ancestral nations. Yes, they were your founding nations, but what they found was this nation. America. Be American. "I'm one-quarter Irish, one-quarter Scottish, one-quarter Dutch, one-qua ..." That's six quarters. What the fuck are you on about? You're all quarters American.

Anyway, back to the Irish bar. I wipe the frosted window clean and cup my hands, ready to gaze through with hopeful anticipation of peeping in on a New York equivalent of Britain's greatest exported bastion. Disbelief, confusion, and a total lack of inculcation drains me. Vacancy adhered to near every seat in the venue, bereft of custom. Yet outside, sidewalk pedestrians dodge a small crowd of shirted patrons shivering in random association around a sand-filled, Home Depot, terra-cotta pot with a cigarette-butt porcupine hibernating on top. Compelled to question, I approach the dandy dressed hoboes about their exiled commune.

I was nearly levelled by the honest retort provisioned to me by the upstanding members of the New York society, who explained the rulings passed by the city to abolish the most innocuous and least threatening of available vices, banishing these mutual and innocent contributors to the gutter. Traitorous government had derived that smoking was no longer to be tolerated in any New York City entertainment establishment. A travesty of reasoning. This city has built a reputation on the holocaust of all things cowardly and irresolute. Leave the sun-bleached Californians to dangerously meddle with public opinion. Let them succumb to their sycophantic pretensions. The prohibition of smoking works in the *fuckville* society of reticence that they elect to live in. New York, however, is a vastly different story.

Light-fingered bureaucratic pickpockets have fleeced New York City of one of its truly civilized cultures, and this is an act of considerable regression. New York has propelled itself to be the most salient of cities; be this by design or by default is of no consequence. The fact remains that this city has to provide an assumed standard and style of living, portrayed by an innumerate number of movies, thousands of written words, and the significant opinions of people more important than me, with stronger and more qualified opinions than mine. New York obliges a guarantee of probable promise with every admission ticket that is sold. New York trades on the reputation that the next street corner hides a fissure of iniquity or a caveat of new and novel insinuation. The retention of this perception requires exclusive and passionate commitment towards preserving this truth and reality. You sell the doubtless fantasy that something good is going to happen to you, tonight, and in this town. You sold it to me. Everybody knows it, and everybody knows that smoking is a small, yet integral, aspect of that. You can't cheat on people with this silent reformation now. I can't believe that you allowed penitence to the suits and the do-gooders at head office. You shouldn't have let them get away with this. *"The city that never sleeps." "So good they named it twice."* Welcome to New York, the greatest city on the face of the earth—but do you mind not smoking? And can you take your shoes off at the front doormat, please? And can you put your drink on a coaster for me? I don't want it to stain.

Be careful, New York. And we'll say no more about it. If you need me, I'll be outside—smoking.

#2: Flick Chicks

Before I left Britain to fumble and forage in this great city, I was informed by a number of impotently qualified resources that the "all-American girl" was an absolute slinky for an accent. And other than Daisy Duke, you can't get much more all-American than a New York chick. So will my days of choiceless chastity be banished from my circulation, with the same magnitude that this free-willing society has banished a word like "chastity" from its literal circulation? I wonder, are New York chicks really so shallow or so drunk as to believe that as diminutive an entity as a foreign tone may potentially fulfill their unfulfilled female aspiration and sophistication? Could my carnal utopia be found in this town and afford to me my undeserved reward, with the use of a celestial caveat that has cost me nothing? Is it possible that my geographic birthplace and mandatory culture might be an asset, where it was once drowned with replication, here it is not? Is it really true that a more refined foreign lisp would be enough to disguise and destroy my countless and undeniably blemished failings, which are latently concealed behind my verbal demeanour?

No!

Despite some very encouraging reconnaissance from my pioneers, I can sadly lay this misnomer to definitive rest: absolutely no New York girls are in the least bit entrapped by a British twang. Or at least not *my* British twang. There were very positive early signs, one in particular, and then nothing until the other day when a *never-gunna-happen,* fat, black, checkout chick made a nice comment in

Bottle King. At first she thought that I was from Australia and then from Germany. There was no third guess.

In fact, the first early signs were fantastic and verified profusely the preparatory reports that I wanted so much to believe. Straight from the touched-down aeroplane, I neglected to drop off my bags and instead debated which location of first-night hedonism to attend with a buddy, who had obliged the errand of an airport run. I was in a fervent mood and eager to dispense with any debilitating jetlag and section my British enunciation to learn if this really was the golden ticket that my sorry existence had dreamed of. Outside the Irish bar, I have a small dalliance to beautify and prepare: I apply a deviously slithered layer of cherry lip balm—*there may be kissing requested later*—though I stop short of using a pocketsize canister of breath spray, instead opting to drop a couple of tic tacs. Minty fresh breath and low in calories. Genius. Now suitably refined in my facial aesthetics, posture, language, behaviour, and above all, my all-empowering British prominence, I stride into the bar with vigilant eyes, spying and endorsing which girls will want to be procured by the currency of charm for my harem.

The going is slow at first. There are few biters being lured by my verbal bait. But, as I have been assured, when my foreign tones enchant the New York girl, this mythical perception will intoxicate her enough to advance with genuine intent in my direction. Everybody is taking it slow. However, I feel that I am being crowded out. The robust, abrasive nature of the native male is perilously invading my scenery. Their excessively loud brashness is contaminating the field. Still, this seems to be very much more effective than my lame, reserved approach. His public display of cell phone conversation with absent parties is drawing more female attention than my subtle dignitaries. But of course! The naivety of me. The strongest of America's capitalist philosophies is to advertise—you may have the best product in the world, but if no fucker knows about it, then who cares? And so there is a change in my game plan. You got to advertise; you got to get out there, kid.

I had lost the jump on a couple of *mooks*, but I was determined that my trump card was enough to take the hand of a queen and win this deal. I raise my volume a few important notches and "English" it up a bit for the benefit of the cameras. On the ladder of social hierarchy, I am now speaking with an accent hammed up enough to put me third in line for the reign of most European countries and at a volume level that can compete with the vulgarity of the competitively conceited American man.

Bingo! Finally, something Wombles my way. Hoist. Serve. Ace. Advantage, Jonny. A very cute siren with a low-cut dress and matching integrity—a veritable honey—slinks over to me and immediately toys with the hook that my accent has maliciously laced. I could not believe it; decisively, the good Lord above had blessed my forgotten time. Me and my amorous accent had been in New York City for about three-quarters of one hour, and already the chicks were flicking. Buoyed by immaculate confidence from my newfound divine assurance, I started to do the math. I've been in the country for forty-five minutes and already I've got one girl. Let's call it an hour. So, I'm in New York for an eighteen-month contract, so that's sixty minutes multiplied by twenty-four hours, multiplied by seven days, multiplied by seventy-seven weeks multipli … Just how many chicks am I going get?

I've been in New York a little over four months now … and I'm still on one. I have concluded that I peaked a little too early. I should have saved her till about around Christmas; something like that. Or maybe until an occasion that required a date.

The muse status rumoured about a British accent hosting in New York is a fabrication of the truth on a grand and potentially embarrassing scale. Impressed, she is not. The opinion of this betrayed little foreign boy is that the New York chick couldn't give a shit.

I didn't really need failure as affirmation that the New York chick wouldn't be fooled by something as insignificant as an accent; all that was just a hopeful dream that I thought maybe could happen. Understanding what the New York chick isn't fooled by is easy. However, understanding what the New York chick is fooled by, or rather what she actually wants, remains an enigma that NASA, Microsoft, one whole gender, and I cannot resolve. All this resource and can I find a date in New York City? Impossible. A prank fraudulent telephone number, a fake e-mail address, or a slap across the cheek, are all very easy—all a bit too easy. But a date? No, no, no. Not for me.

Why not me? I've got game. I've tried being things that I am not; I've tried clothes; I've tried money; I've tried hair. You know what? I've even tried being me. Being me was a decision based on skewed advice though. A 4:00 AM martini-fuelled conversation with a lesbian friend. I motion right now that all lesbian friends should be abolished from male compatibility. No exceptions. I hate the lesbian friend. Trying to learn advice about a gender from someone who has total sexual awareness and complete neurosis understanding of that gender is futile. Are you telling me just to be myself? Unfortunately *myself* is not identical to *themselves*. *Myself* does not have the total sexual awareness and complete neurosis understanding of the gender, so in all honesty, *myself* is the last thing that they are looking for. Be myself? Be you, my lesbian friend, is what I should be.

Women are not bad people; they are not, and I truly believe that. New York chicks, especially, have a fantastically strong and desirable oxymoronic trait of laconic congeniality. I confess that this is tantalizingly attractive. It is just that at nearly every turn, I see New York chicks, with whom I would bypass conversation to propose instant monogamous marriage, flirting with boorish local males who choose to wear their shirts tucked into their high waistbands of mother-ironed beige slacks that fall at least an inch short of black polished loafers to reveal the chosen accessory of white sport socks. I don't mind so much being defeated by the better man—I have respect for the better man. But, come on, chicks of New York. By what rules and of what game are we playing here? Help me out.

One explanatory thought from a school of sobriety about my alluring lack of fascination by the New York chick is this: You know the heart-sunken, worthless, underachieving sensation suffered when a girl far too far out of attracting range walks into a bar? A girl just too sensational unwittingly flirts with the extremities of your world—a chick way too slinky that it would be just futile for you to risk indignity trying to tempt. A girl undoubtedly too complex and insatiably demanding that you remain seated, deceiving defeat before the contest can even commence. You know this girl? Well, maybe that's what I've got. Maybe I'm just too enchanting, too special, and New York chicks are thinking that there's no chance even speculating with me. Maybe they think that it's never going to happen with me.

Well, it just might, if you ask. I remain open and optimistic. And I remain still British.

#3: Twelve Little Honeys

The favourite soccer team that I coach in New York is by far and away my diminutive little angels. I have the privilege and accountability to deliver the development curriculum to an under-ten girl's soccer team in small-town Jersey. I spend my days teaching stepovers and squeezy pushes to an eight-a-side bunch of girls with nine-year-old smiles. The honour is enchanting. The company of children is a funny thing, and to be blessed with a squad of twelve little honeys makes for the most delicious companionship and is time very much well spent. Twice a week they come to me for soccer tutelage in hour-and-a-half training sessions wearing a tiny little soccer uniform, carrying a tiny little soccer ball and arriving only a tiny little bit late. I have yet to find a better ninety minutes in all the world.

However, once at soccer training, the tone of infancy changes. These soccer machines, undivided in their pursuit of soccer excellence, leave cute decorum at the edge of the field. Cleats are sharpened and game faces drawn, as combat is imminent. The effort and ethic that my girls express is unprecedented; blood, sweat, and someone else's tears are given to exhaustion each and every time. The reward for this graft is the deliverance of a Sunday game-day spanking, as opposition teams are ruined with lessons of soccer schooling—sixty minutes of persistence, with no variation or compassion. Only at the final whistle do they then return to nine-year-old child perfection.

Unforgivably, there are of course times where resistance to their age and to their gender just cannot be supplied, and submissive soccer training becomes a much failed second to more captivating activities of nine-year-old interest. Too many times, I must abandon my professionally prepared and intricate motivational halftime team talk. My tactical and elaborate seminar on how to exploit a weakened defensive unit will often be neglected for curiosity over an unsuitably placed earthworm, a flying bug of stinging potential, or sibling petulance. Having twins on your team is not always of benefit.

Cuddly toys and teddy bears fill kit bags as often as shin guards and cleats. Pre-game superstitions are simply for all to touch a furry green puppet or a rubber duck. "Patty you didn't touch the frog!" "Oh, Sorry." A fulltime synopsis of on-field errors is dismissed, as confectionary, play dates, and sleepovers become the main priority now. Post game rituals are not to watch documentary analysis of next week's opponents and to plan training sessions on how to deal with their busy left-winger. The nine-year-old conclusion of a game simply treasures a pool party. "Your pool or mine? Did you bring your swimmers?" Powers of recovery are monumental. Occasional defeats are crippling to take and can grieve me for days if genuinely harsh. I'll be dealing with this one until Wednesday. Nine-year-old innocence can deem a score line forgotten in less than fifteen minutes. "Did you win or lose?" "Yeah, I played okay."

The end-of-season extravaganza is a pizza party. Ray's Pizza Parlour lines three tables end to end, and the girls file in with disorder and noise. In the commotion, I think one girl might even have fallen over; I'm not quite sure. Seeing as nine-year-old girls are made of rubber, she's up and at the table with limited fuss, so I don't even know if it happened or not. Pitchers of sugar-rush soda are ordered, and two of Sprite are delivered in double-quick time, accompanied by a tower of plastic beakers. Before the pitcher of Coke arrives, two glasses of lemonade are knocked over and drain to the floor through the crack in the tables. Twelve girls, all the associated younger and older sisters, and a couple of gate-crash kids have bunted the numbers to uncontrollable proportions. Children and mess and more noise are evident and everywhere. Two are in the restroom running faucets, one is in the dry store, a couple are under the table, a couple are under someone else's table, and one got into the kitchen, only to be escorted out by a laconic chef. Forget the education of the offside rule; this is hard.

Less than observant parents dismiss the childhood anarchy, assigning responsibility to the waitress or to myself. My responsibility of them is on a soccer field. I am weak and powerless off it, and I have no authority outside of straight white lines. Pizza parlour discipline is well out of my remit here. Can somebody help, please? Tepid pizza is delivered with the absence of toppings; pepperoni and bacon is not the chosen cuisine of a nine-year-old girl. Slices are distributed on paper plates, and more napkins are required. To my dismay, the butchery of pizza is ubiquitously performed. Each girl removes the cheese and tomato from her given slice and places it in a molten pile of debris next to a paper plate; not on a paper plate, you understand, but next to a paper plate. Little dairy volcanoes are everywhere. All that remains is pizza base with the vague semblance of pizza. We have all come to a pizza parlour, and nobody is willing to eat pizza. As far as I am concerned, they are all just eating bread. This is not a pizza party; this is a bread party. I'm at a nine-year-old girls' end-of-soccer-season bread party.

Carnage is beyond my control. I can only salvage so much mess and disrupt so many problems; this task is above me. In retort to the waitress's disgruntled gaze, I declare defeat, and I declare ignorance. Sorry, lady, I have never seen any of these people before in my life. However, I begin to comprehend the paternal approach to such an event. I think that the tactic is to let the girls make as much confusion and turmoil as they are going to and then just clear up at the end. Endure and then tidy.

The soccer management of nine-year-old girls is an eventful and enjoyable task in equal proportion. However, the management of the American soccer parent is a different world altogether. The definition of *parent* could be exchanged for *agent*, following post-match analysis and conversation. A more blinkered perception of ability and contribution will be hard to find. I respect a parental interest in the development of their child, I really do, and this is a healthy thing; it is just that sometimes perspective is lost to negligent proportions. It's nine-year-old girls soccer that we are dealing with. Never forget that.

I think maybe that overly analytical American parents are compensating for the less-than-disinterested parents of British latchkey kids. A British parent would not confront a soccer coach following a disgruntled playing time grievance; a phone call would not be made with the incentive of procuring a starting berth or first-team selection. Dissention does not exist in Britain, and reproach lies squarely at the feet of the player. A player's failure is most definitely their own responsibility.

The American parent seems to associate the fear of failure with themselves more than most. My kid can't fail, because it's my kid. I like the interest and I like the involvement that is miles in advance of a British parent; it is just that the manifestation of resolution seems often warped. If a kid gets benched, then the American parent feels the indignity is an insult to them and not to their player.

Game-day results are of minor relevance for my tiny players, where the pursuit of soccer excellence is priority. So a benched player is often a sign of rotation and not the reflection of failing. This is sometimes a difficult ticket to sell to an irate and repeatedly misinformed parent.

I think the aggressive attitude that some American parents can display concerning their little players is good, if aggression can be tempered into commitment instead. What I do find odd is that the answer to commitment is to pay for someone to solve the problem, where perhaps more parenting would return a greater dividend. Frequently the less capable players are the goof-off kids who have behavioural and disciplinary problems. Rarely is the problem the session planning of the coach.

The scapegoat of responsibility is often someone other than the parent, the most salient candidate being the coach. But it will never be the kid. However, in America there are other bizarre entities in the frame for accountability, including mental irregularity. Attention Deficit Disorder is the language of the weak and is the cause of every behavioural problem possible. In Britain, ADD does not exist, and quite rightly so. How dare a parent assign responsibility to such an intangible and vague entity?

I think it odd that an American parent would rather their child be diagnosed mentally irregular than lazy.

#4: Jew Ball

Back home in Britain, soccer is the only religion that is worshiped, and over here in New York, I was under the impression that your religion was food. New York is all about the food! The truth is, it's not.

From what I see, your religion is ... well, it's still religion. Misdirected for a while, I prejudged that the culinary choice to be bathed in the most significance by the New Yorker would be pizza, and I would not have argued with that appraisal in the slightest. The pizza available from numerous reputable vendors gives huge testament to the integrity of catering in this town. I have spent many a happy 2:00 AM vigil hanging at the counter, being served by the irreverent, smutty, apron-wearing, rotund proprietor, whose name stands high and proud above his shop. Don't get me wrong, we do have pizza back home—everybody does. This Italian simplicity has rightly become a staple in many cultures. But, there is something just a little bit blessed about the way a New York pepperoni piece of pie slides over to you on overlapping paper plates, with too few napkins to resist the flowing trail of cheese juice, which I gamble will be on your shirt sleeve before you make that corner table. A masterstroke of bypassed evolution and wisdom. Why not buy bigger plates? No, just use two.

I love the tray of condiments that maintenance forgot, usually located above the garbage can, the misnomer of selection galore. One shaker of dried chili flakes, all now too big to fit through the holes, and five shakers of parmesan that are on a dubious stock rotation scheme. Do we trust it? Fuck it; it's only Listeria. Oregano or ganja? Can't tell.

I find it very difficult to comprehend how, with having to achieve a genuine gross profit margin, these guys can sell gigantic slices of pizza and still get out of town with a three dollar charge. The required supplies alone, as minimal as they are, must surely cost more than the asking price, let alone the overheads—the rent, bills, and bungs, and the wages of the bloke who drives around the '84 Honda Civic delivering tepid pizza and sitting on top of the chest freezer learning English during quiet times.

These places are ubiquitously devoid of hygiene. I personally don't care. That's why I like them. I'm not trying to get anyone closed down or nothing; far from it. I think a lower standard of hygiene is to be encouraged, unless of course we are talking about night ladies of relaxed carnal integrity, in which case high standards of hygiene are mandatory. But we're not; we're talking about complacent pizza shops, so knock yourself out. Blasé away. Only in some of the more remote locations of contemporary Eastern Europe have I witnessed a greater mitigation of the proper procedures for food preparation, and I loved it there as well. Kitchens are an impossible industry to keep squeaky clean, even those windows that boast Michelin accreditations aren't as shiny on the inside as you might hope. Read a Tony Bourdain text. So you're fucked if you think that the slice-a-minute side-street gypsy is going to sweep behind his vegetable fridge every night–'cuz he isn't. These people recognize that you can go overboard on cleanliness, and so they don't. Sanitary insanity. Try writing that at 2:01 AM, while using your one soiled napkin to blot a grease spot off your favourite white Diesel shirtsleeve.

Anyway, as we have already discussed, food is not the New York religion; religion is. Which makes all that pizza stuff pretty much irrelevant. So what's the crossover? The crossover is this: In Britain, soccer is the one truly important entity, and in the United States, your epiphany is still the epiphany, and New York provisions me the fated miscarriage of both.

Soccer should be called football and is done so by every other coherent nation on the planet, with the exceptions of the isolated Australians and the narcissistic Americans. How I would love it for you to call it football. I concede that I am failing in this futile pursuit to change you. Football in Britain has a very different heritage and origin from that of the history of U.S. soccer. In fact, the odysseys of British football against that of it in the United States are aggressively at the antitheses of each other. Football in Britain is an urban, inner-city, working class salvation. Born to the never-to-be-gentrified decay, you are given fewer and fewer options for deliverance; either work the mines or the heavy shipbuilding industry, or find enough passion to play your way out from oppression. This is the undeniable adolescence of the game back home. Glasgow, Newcastle, Manchester, Liverpool, and London are all the richest soccer seams for clear reason. I suppose U.S. basketball is its most incestuous relation mirrored over here.

So I degrade my religion to New York. I pay my bills and generate my flash money coaching the obstinate juveniles of New Jersey. Do you think that I am afforded the naturally athletic, devoted child, the ardent soccer kid, the diamond who is kicking and screaming and scratching and fighting his way out of the street? No, no I am not. The heredity—the very heart and soul of soccer—over here has been removed and replaced with money and middle-class affluence. Instead, I get to work with the fat Jewish kid who has a disinterested father in fatherhood who chooses to redeem paternal responsibility with Manhattan-earned dollars. I don't get the street survivor who can sprint the distance in eleven seconds, but I have to try to triumph with the raw material that can only attend practice if it doesn't clash with a clarinet recital or with being tailored for a double-breasted bar mitzvah suit. And by the way, the kid can't play on Fridays because of Hebrew school, and he'll miss a whole year of under-thirteen tryouts because every other Saturday will be committed to somebody's coming-of-age party.

The conversation between a British soccer coach pursuing his graft in New York and a malevolently rich Jewish parent at desperate measures and financial means for his son to learn some ball skills is disheartening.

"Make young Joshua good at soccer."

"In all honesty, I can't. I can make him better, but I can't make him good."

"Make young Joshua good at soccer."

"I can't."

"Make young Joshua good at soccer. I've got money."

"It's not about money. Just face it; he's never going to be a player. He's going to be an … accountant."

"I've got money."

"Money can't cheat biology."

"I've got money."

"It really doesn't matter."

"I've got money."

"Stop saying that."

It's not a racist thing; it's just a thing that the Jewish are not that good at soccer. There are no strong role models; Jewish is just not a centre of soccer excellence. It's not wrong; it's just that religion is more dedicated than sport.

The game day sideline coaching of an all-Jewish soccer team is a humbling existence. It is sorrowing to have your perfectly coordinated flat back four contorted out of position by plump Jewish ineptitude, more interested in refusing defensive responsibilities in order to retrieve their ground fallen skull caps, while gleeful Hispanic kids dance easily beyond, questioning whether this inevitable score will be four or five unanswered goals before the halftime intermission.

"I've got money."

Fuck off. Go and take the kid out for dinner and tell him how the family business is run. Three dollars will buy him a quality slice of pizza, and seven dollars will get his shirtsleeve dry cleaned.

#5: Are You Shore?

The sunny weekend vocation for the New York soccer family is to forget the summer select program that the soccer academy offers and head for the golden bleached beaches of the Jersey shore.

For me the summer is a time for out-of-season tournament soccer, where the most committed of players from individual soccer clubs are *selected* to form champagne teams to play the elite game under the academy sponsorship and without the jeopardy of the soccer club coaching contract. My little honeys choose to negate such an invitation and opt for the vanilla blond miles of the Atlantic-lapped North Jersey coastline. No weekend soccer tournament in Pennsylvania can ever really hope to compare to inflatable armbands, cookouts, and beach mischief.

I have been down the Jersey shore before. Last time we went to the youth beaches of Point Pleasant and occupied the slinky bars for most of the afternoon. Not being much of a beach comfortable tenant I was happy with the bar scene, but I was pretty much of the opinion that I have been to the shore once and so that was enough. The city is where it's really at.

The affluence of the soccer moms, and more accurately the soccer dads, hides secret summer residences and beach club memberships at covert locations all the way along the Atlantic rim. When offered an invitation to meet up with the family of one of my little honeys at the beach house, I stop and ponder and then decline such an altruistic offer. The gesture is genuine and understood in much the same way, but the beach really isn't my sort of thing. While the company of the family would be delicious, I have to refuse with an elegant "no." The retort is not accepted; the invitation has been delivered, and now delivery of appearance is not just expected but positively compulsory. Friends and relatives have been prematurely contacted and all are delighted that the soccer coach will be in attendance at the weekend festivities, and reticence from me would only disappoint Auntie Nora, potentially to her grave.

Fuck, this is out of hand already. I'm due to meet relatives. At best I was hoping for a lazy, booze-up at the beach, and now I have to meet all sorts of people. I bet I get palmed off on Auntie Nora all day. Reluctantly, I accept my invitation and send my grateful acceptance of such a privilege. The itinerary of events is e-mailed through to me. Hang on. Itinerary of events. What? Are we not just going to drink it up all day?

No.

8:30 AM–9:30 AM: Individual soccer coaching lesson for Patsy and Brian.

Now hang on a minute; stop the fuck there. No one said anything about a soccer lesson, and no one said anything about 8:30 AM. I live fifty minutes from the beach, so if you think that I'm driving down the parkway for that time in the morning, then somebody has something very much wrong, and it ain't me.

I put the phone call through immediately and yet find myself powerless to resist the family program. "I'll be there a little before, if that's okay." What the fuck am I talking about?

My Saturday night of hedonism is ruined for a Sunday morning voyage. I jump in the company motor and head for the parkway south. Two tolls and junction number 107 are negotiated with consummate ease. I am supposed to be fuelling the car with self-paid gasoline, but that sentiment has gone far out the window. Work-expense gas is paid for out of company coffers and a pooled slush fund from employees; personal usage is deemed personal. Many abuse such a selfless concession and milk a few yards onto the company tab. My last gas bill was in very much excess of a trip down the shore and so I sneak my private journey onto the communal bill without a bead of guilt. Fully loaded and racing the miles, I hit the exit in unprecedented time.

Despite inadequate directions, I negotiate to the beach house at the appointed rendezvous, and I alight with a tandem stretch and yawn. No time for that. Straight to the soccer field for the private lesson. It's half past eight in the morning, for fuck's sake. What are you doing to me? The morning Jersey sun is penetrating as I play out a perfect private soccer lesson and sweat out the cans of beer that I drank in the house last night.

9:30 AM: Collect Auntie Nora and head for the beach club.

I shower back at the beach house and dress in what I consider beachwear: jeans, a dress shirt, sunglasses, and sandals. Everyone else has shorts and a T-shirt, with swimmers underneath, including Auntie Nora. And all are distressed to hear that I will not be needing swimmers, including Auntie Nora. I'm not going into any pool; I'm not going into any ocean; I will not be sunbathing; and so I will not need any shorts, and I will definitely not be needing any swimmers.

There are a couple of reasons why I hold such strong reticence to swimming with the family. The first and most important is that I don't really like swimming; I'm not the biggest fan of getting wet so stop fucking asking me to do so. The second reason is that my connection to the family is that of the soccer coach to the under-ten girls team that has brought us all together, and so for both professional reasons and for personal reasons, I think it best not to be seen frolicking around with nine-year-old, bikini-clad girls in a communal swimming pool. The third and most salient reason is that I think it most inappropriate for my nine-year-old, god-blessed soccer player to witness the religious ridiculing and anti-Semitic tattoo that adorns my back and that took many sessions at the parlour to complete. So if it's all the same to everybody, I'm just going to sit at the bar, if that's okay? So, you won't go to swim in the pool–let's go and swim in the ocean. No, that's still water.

The beach club has a vast, wide, and safe area of private sand with a haven of small cabins horseshoed around. The cabins are full of amenities, and the decked patios leaves lazy parents to view the children at play. The beach club representative approaches with a familiar smile, and the memorable handshake confirms my perception. I am demanded of my preference on a case of beer and immediately attempt to absolve any decision-making responsibility with a vague reply. I truly don't care. A split case of Corona and Coors Light is ordered, as I affirmed that I was in favour of both of these brands. I appreciate your altruism, but please don't get this stuff just for me. The beer seemed excessive, particularly since I was having to drive back home at the end of the evening; the purchase was made with me in mind all the same.

The kids ran from the pool to the ocean and back to the pool again, only ever checking in with the parents to collect money for the Pepsi machine or for reapplications of sun lotion. I was sat on the deck in the shade, drinking Corona and

Coors Light, reading my book, and turning up my jeans in a vain effort to address the tan lines of my ankles.

2:30 PM: Circulate for drinks.

At half past two everything starts to move around a little. The male head of each cabin family rises from the sun bed and begins a reunion tour of each neighbouring cabin, socializing and asking after the welfare of the contiguous relatives. Each visit is only one drink in duration and then with a clockwork departure, empty wine glasses are jettisoned, and the next family is embraced. It was perfect. Everyone just moving around—take a drink, leave a drink, and have a chat. Hang on a minute—if he's going to be getting a drink at each and every one of these cabins, then I need to be a part of that. "Hi there, I'm Jonny. I'm the soccer coach. Gin and tonic, please."

4:25 PM: Male-only drinks at the adjacent beach club bar.

With no noticeable initiation, each male of a required age has congregated for a masse exodus towards the bar for some more drinks and to ogle a few tasty moms, while their own tasty mom was now in responsibility of sole supervision. Nobody knows what these women get up to while the men are away. And nobody ever asks. I tried to reciprocate a few drinks of gratitude at the bar, but I was not allowed to do so. I was finding it very difficult to get my hand in my pocket for anything. MILF count very high!

6:00 PM: Barbeque.

Beach club rules mandate that no barbeque cooking can take place before six o'clock. It maximizes the potential of punting out in-house catering, I suppose. Anyway with the curfew abolished a frenzied activity consumes all cabins, as male-dominated cooking takes place. Big-arsed, gas-powered grills are flamed to the top setting, and loads of meat are instantly singed while racist jokes are told out by burley men holding Cosmopolitans and spatulas, smoking cigars, and wearing pointless and effeminate aprons. Kids flash in and out to grab at hot dog sausages and cardboard burgers that have gone too far. The jokes are not tempered, given the innocent ears.

The children run themselves till dark before they are scooped up in mothering arms and fall asleep, resting on a comfortable shoulder, finally beaten by the sun and perhaps beaten by some of that Cosmopolitan they pilfered outside of paternal reprimand. The wives take the kids home to the beach house and the husbands see out the quiet night smoking cigars and thinking about their families. A few take the opportunity to nap a while.

It was time for me to leave and to make the parkway trip home, so I collected my belongings and said my grateful good-byes. As I depart, there is an attempt to pay me for my hour of soccer coaching from the morning's individual session. I decline the money. Soccer coaching is my profession, and usually an hour of private tuition earns me sixty dollars. But after a day of free booze, all the food you can eat, and perhaps more importantly, after admission into a family environment that all the money in the world could not buy for me or my absent family, the work just did not deserve a price. Today I got paid with a cathartic currency.

As I was driving home, I took from my bag a packet of cigarettes that had been teasing me all afternoon, but smoking was the one activity that I just could not be seen to employ. It doesn't do for a professional soccer coach to be smoking around his kids. He shouldn't really be smoking at all, but then that's another issue. When I replaced the cigarettes, I noticed a wedge of money marking a page of my book. I removed the money and counted out seventy dollars in a fold of notes. They had sneaked the money on me and done so with a tip. Some people are just too good to you.

The next day I put through a phone call and thanked them for a fantastic day, and I thanked them for the money, which I would be returning to them in complimented individual soccer tuition. The reply was dismissive of the returning money, but promising with new opportunity. Apparently the individual soccer tuition was an attractive proposal to many of the neighbouring cabin dwellers, and they had placed requisitions for my professional time on my next return to the beach house. Five new sessions had been arranged for the following Sunday, six when you include my complimented session. These five sessions had not been sold at the recommended retail price of sixty dollars an hour, not even sold at the inflated price of seventy dollars an hour, but at an unprecedented ninety dollars an hour. Call it a finder's fee. "What? Are you sure?"

On the following Sunday I went to the beach house and delivered five individual soccer coaching sessions, six when you include my complimented session, and earned $450.00 on the day, not including the booze, the food, and the family. I should have paid out $10.00 in petrol and so in reality had cleared $460.00 for six hours work, and my pocket was as affluent as it had been in a long time.

On the drive back home I reached to my bag to locate my cigarettes and noticed a fold of notes marking a page of my book. About seventy dollars.

#6: Quit Buggy'ing Me

A premature commitment on my behalf left me with my misjudgement to represent the team in an end-of-season soccer club charity event around eighteen holes of a classy Jersey golf course. I have always contrived myself to be a little distant from golf and the community of social regulation that it carries. I would not say that my reticence was founded on intimidation for the sport or even that of the players, but golf definitely commands my scepticism. So the reason why I volunteered to slaughter my dignity in such an erroneous forum still remains absent. A more considered approach would have been prudent. What I do have to consider now is how to get round without having any semblance of ability or decorum.

Closer scrutiny of the invitation reads that obedience of full course rules and convention is mandatory and enforceable with financial penalty. Charity event. Too fucking true. This is going to cost me more than the $180.00 that I foolishly boasted at ten bucks a hole. Deliverance of victory just does not marry well with my vulnerable tendency for a gamble.

Rapid Internet research provides a ten-page document contaminated with little pieces of inconvenience, which I need to resolve in order to get on the first tee without a fine. Rule number two: golf shoes. Who the fuck has golf shoes anymore? Golfers do. This is handy, however, as rule number one stated that I have to have golf clubs as well. I can just ask the golfing Samaritan who was going to lend me their sticks if I can pinch their shoes. They should say yes, because there is very little cause for a person to require their golf shoes if they don't even have their golf clubs, and they're not playing golf. I need to borrow a lot of stuff.

Equipment is just one thing, mind you; actual game play understanding is another that is more delicate to solicit.

Fuck it. If you look good enough, then they will believe that you can play. This was a poor assumption. I like your sentiment, kid, but you know, it just ain't gonna work.

A six o'clock alarm call is ridiculous, even for a World Cup game, but for golf this is extremely depressing. We load the cumbersome equipment into the car and commence the drive to the clubhouse. A lot of people seem very vibrant for this time in the morning; their assurance sees them greater convinced in their preparation and ability. I am lost. And we haven't even started yet.

First hole: 453 yards. What the fuck are you on about—453 yards? How far is that? I can't even see where I'm supposed to finish up in four shots' time. I'm standing there with the putter over my shoulder. There are no windmills anywhere; no clowns or tricky passageways to get through—the first hole should be a simple two-cushion escape around an L-turn. Three yards maximum, par two, with the second shot a five-inch gimme if your angles were good off the tee.

For me crazy golf is exactly where golf needs to place itself. Anything more serious than that and golf just should not be able to find room in a cultured society. However, real golf has one salvation for its prolonged existence, and I have to admit right here that the one salvation that golf does have is a very strong one. The golf buggy is a masterstroke of interest-retaining brilliance. More entertainment was redeemed from driving the buggy than can ever be offered from driving a ball—into some trees.

My four started our first tee on the thirteenth hole, which meant a good two-mile buggy road race through the winding course. Overtaking manoeuvres are near impossible when the lead buggy has the jump on you. They have absolutely no pickup, and the acceleration is crap. Cornering is very tight, and the track designer offered very few passing opportunities. You would be surprised how much fun you can have at twelve miles an hour.

Golfing etiquette is a world that I did not care to address before I took a weighty five wood out of the bag and perched my Titleist 3 on a small yellow tee about an inch off the ground. Whatever I needed to know, I would pick up along the way. Others chose to stretch a little in preparation, and they questioned my absence to do so. One man, one shot. Here we go. I settled my grip on the shaft and shuffled my feet, ensuring that someone else's shoes had my required assurance of stability. My eyes ranged from ball to fairway and then to the ball once more. My back lift was smooth and elegant. I could feel the doubters begin to replace their assumptions. A natural genius? Better check your wallets to see if you can cover your bets. My head was still and my left arm as rigid as the advice that I adhered to. I held the apex with perfect form; I think one person even took a photograph for a textbook. The downswing was rapid and whistled with power in pursuit of the ball. There was nothing in the world that could now prevent a two hundred and ten yard drive to the centre of the fairway. My ball was surely gone. Surely.

I connected with the ground nearly a foot behind the desired destination, sending a divot forward faster then the authorities were sending me a bill for green fees. I replaced a piece of grass so big that a family could have set up a picnic on it. The jarring of my wrist started to turn into an odd numbing sensation down my left side. Stroke. Maybe you should try a four iron or a five iron. Fuck your four iron and your five iron. I could swing a cast iron clothes iron and I still don't think that it would make a lot of difference. Quit bugging me.

I set up for a second swing and sliced it sideways with contradictory geometric proportions, which threatened the welfare of adjacent players. Protocol demands that some warning or cautionary notification be offered to implicated players in such a predicament. Simply out of morbid curiosity I negated the standard counsel call of *"four"* instead choosing to witness and then accept any consequence of injuries caused. Seven shots over. Eleven scored.

The game of golf was quickly losing its charm with me, which was a detrimental thing, as it never even began with any charm. Eighteen holes was looking like fifteen too many. Sporadic moments of aptitude were all too frequently punctuated with mulligans lost in the pond, lost in the trees, or sunk in a bunker that you have to rake afterward just to insult your failing. At least by the tenth hole, most had also lost their own faith in the game, and buggy mischief was now a higher priority than a clean scorecard. Fabricated buggy crashes; thick rough safaris and a game of trust with the water hazard were better ways of occupying time.

An old guy in his own buggy came driving round with SECURITY printed on the side. Rule 54: Buggies can only enter the fairway at 90 degrees. Yeah, whatever mate. I never read past rule five, did I? Handbrake turn. He didn't actually catch us during a moment of infraction, but how good a job is it to be the security officer on a golf course?

A few holes later and a concessions buggy came round with a hostess vending chips and drinks and confectionary. What is all this? There could be a whole community of buggy driving golf course dwellers that I just never knew existed.

There could be old crappy beaten up buggies that golf pizza delivery drivers drive and golf physics teachers ridicule to school in. There could be a big yellow buggy that golf Otto drives and contra flow buggies have to wait while golf school kids alight. There could be pimped up buggies that golf black dudes drive and golf ghetto criminals break into during the golf night; a smelly golf garbage buggy that doesn't come around on public holidays, but will not inform anybody of the change in schedule; a big square pink golf ice cream buggy; a buggy breakdown buggy.

Eighteenth hole embracement was abandoned by all, as the clubhouse balcony whispered the breeze with laughter, catering, and the bar. The clubs were jettisoned in quick time, and pitchers were ordered. Frothy topped perfection somehow had the gift to console our early start, our now absent four hours, and the degrading realization of inability. I shot somewhere near one hundred and fifty. Accurate documentation does not exist, so you will just have to trust me on this one. The better players were going round in the eighties and nineties. Judging by the fashion sense on display, I think that everyone went around in the eighties.

My favourite part of the whole day was when I understood that I had participated in something that I hated and that they adored so much, and yet I got to play twice as many shots as they did. How can a sport reward the pursuit of excellence with reduced playing time? The better you get, the less you get to play. I was crap and could have been out there swinging all day while the good players are already at home. Just something for golf to think about.

Golf has a culture back home in Britain, and I think it has an even bigger culture here. I just don't think that it is the culture of this little soccer boy. I liked my time, and I'm glad that I came, but when next year's soccer club charity event comes around, why don't we just play soccer?

#7: Wastepaper Basket Ball

In New York a lot of people have a lot of money, and affluence is very evident. In suburban New Jersey the affluence is even more evident and at times a little more tangible. The more altruistic parents of the kids I coach like to gift a little here and there. Sometimes the motive is genuine altruism, and other times these are sycophantic gestures, an attempt to profit my favour and with it perhaps a starting berth in Sunday's cup game. I stand with morality. You can t buy your way onto my team; you definitely have to play your way in. But I will take a free lunch every now and again. There's no treachery in a Subway sandwich, is there? Ham, turkey, and cheese on whole wheat, please.

My most recent gift was a basketball ticket. I have to concede that I would never demograph myself as a basketball fanatic, but when the opportunity arrives to indulge of a true American culture and participate in something that has meaning to so many, then I feel the acceptance to attend very necessary. If nothing else, I can appreciate professional sport organized in a professional arena and watched by professional supporters. They also have cheerleaders at basketball, and this is only a good thing.

The New Jersey Nets are a pretty decent team and play at the Meadowlands arena, a colossal venue sheltered in the shadow of the even more colossal Giants Stadium. The setup is sensational and the envy of many cities that choose to host a game. I am no American football journalist, but it would appear to the laymen that the Giants' level of game play does not mirror their magnificent home ground; a sand castle rather than a fortress is how the back pages of *The New York Times* reads on Monday morning reflection of Sunday night football. However, the Meadowlands seems to be more charmed, and so my optimism is rife.

The game day ticket is passed to me in a flippant manner, deriding its value and with it the betrayal of many. I am sure that I was not the first on the list to be offered these tickets, but simply the first taker. The printed cover value for the ticket reads at ninety dollars, and we had two. This ticket was pulled from a season ticket book, and though you receive a weakened invoice for your financial promise, the cost of the ticket is still adventurous. And yet it was handed to me with complacency and with no real consideration to the genuine basketball fan.

These tickets belong to a person who is rich enough to afford a season ticket for the basketball, but then they have so much money that they don't even need to go. I find it disgusting. I think that when you buy a ticket for a sporting event, you buy more than just a seat to sit in. I think you buy a responsibility. And that responsibility is commitment. During the game you have the responsibility to support your chosen club; simple attendance is not enough. Attendance is mandatory. Your responsibility is to contribute above and well beyond attendance. The privilege of a ticket is yours; it's not the privilege of the club to collect your dollars.

Okay, I fully concede that any given basketball club plays something like two thousand games in a regular season, and so absenteeism is inevitable—births, deaths, marriage and maybe even work are going to intervene—but, I still don't think that this is fair mitigation as to why I'm holding this ticket, even to an insignificant school-night game. The genuine occupier should be here, or at least *a* genuine occupier should be here.

To make things worse, these tickets were for floor seats. But how good could these tickets be if I have to sit on the floor? They can't be that good if you don't even get a chair. Only a basketball novice would understand this oxymoronic statement with literal meaning. Of course these tickets are the best in the house. We were ushered deep into the viscera of the stadium to be illuminated with seats just one row from the courtside. With a pretty small stick I could have annoyed the benched players with schoolyard mischief. I had no stick, long or short, and even less desire to do so, but I could have. I was that close.

I turned around and craned my neck to watch terrace above terrace ride high behind me, and it felt all wrong. Thousands of supporters—genuine supporters—filled the cheap seats. Not that cheap. Not that cheap at all, actually. Kids with replica shirts, with caps, flags, and passion, screamed from the balconies, near cheating death, being dangled by ankle-gripping fathers that they just might get to touch a hero on his way onto the court. I can touch this hero and all his giant buddies just by leaning over a little, yet the deserving kid who has invested a lifetime must watch from the moon. Fair enough that the arena has perfect sightlines for even the blind, but surely I have this kid's ticket, don't I? I've got his seat. The hero that the kid screams adoringly to could bump into me in the shopping mall and be met with my negligent recognition, only to have me apologize and then curse at him when he's out of hearing distance. Me having this ticket is a waste of paper and a waste of integrity.

I remember watching Cup finals of my favourite soccer team back home and wishing above all else that I could find a golden ticket. It never really happened. I used to spend hours reading soccer magazines, fatiguing my cerebral capacity on irrelevant statistics and trivia that were perfectly pertinent to me at the time. This was my currency. Saturday afternoons I would adorn a whole bedroom wall with posters purchased with pocket money invested over agonizing months. I recall blunting mother's nail scissors, liberated from a dresser drawer, in order to cut with nine-year-old accuracy, smudged newspaper clippings for scrapbooking purposes. I have been there; I know what it's like to be a kid who supports a club. I still am that kid. And how dare somebody rob that kid of his ticket; to rob him of his right. The last person of all it should be is me. I find the whole scenario abhorrent.

Uneasy with the morality of the situation, my tray rests on my knees while I eat dry chicken nuggets and carelessly fried fries and straw suckle a gallon of Coke to beyond gastronomic fulfillment and towards flatulence. Let's consume less and think about the game. Perhaps time to think less and consume the game.

Without trying to condemn a whole industry, I'm of the opinion that basketball is a game of boredom, and that the victorious endeavourer will be the team that manages to resist tedium to the greatest degree. Forty-eight minutes of on-field confrontation is lingered to hours with interruption after unnecessary interruption of strategizing and conceited congratulating and egotistical massaging. The last three minutes of any and every basketball game are the most important, everything else was just a prelude that you didn't really need to see, and these three minutes take thirty-five minutes of actual time—real time and my time—to play.

I am yet to be convinced that basketball players are even proper athletes. I think that they are just tall people. I mean, if you are six foot six, then what else are you going to be other than a basketball player? There's just nothing else that you can do. 6' 6". You *are* going to be a basketball player. And for me that is what detracts from the sport. You don't have to be good; you just have to be tall. At five foot nine and a quarter I could be the best basketball player around; I'm not, but if I were, then some inept giant would still beat me every single time. An off-the-scale shoe size will win you a contract before skill and ability ever will, and that, I think, is wrong. No sport should triumph where physical anomaly is more prevalent than aptitude and talent.

I have to say that basketball did not capture the heart of this little foreigner. I won't speak for a whole planet, but I think I can see why the world does not embrace basketball as one of its treasures to be proud off. Players ailing around a court trying to shoot a hoop just didn't really do that much for me, and all the cheerleading that you can squeeze into a timeout won't change that. Keep trying with the cheerleading thing though.

I found basketball odd to many degrees. Basketball raised a lot of questions for me and sadly drew a lot of disappointment and disparagement. The most salient point that chuckled me the most from my courtside vantage was the way that ten massive black dudes get bossed around by one small white referee. Five foot of Caucasian authority governs in a regime where a black leviathan is king. There's either a joke or a political comment in there somewhere. I'm not sure which yet.

#8: The Fall Guy

I like New York—I sincerely do. But when the opportunity contrived to get out for a night, then I thought that I just might oblige. I'm not betraying the city, and I still want back in the morning, but it's just that I coveted to try something new. When away day soccer games travel me around, I often end up in sleepy Garden State hamlets and rural communities that host a lethargic farmhouse bazaar, quaint bagel stores, and an easy soccer team. This time I was looking for a little bit more sensation than that. What I'm *really* looking for is the adventure of New York, but beyond the city limits of variation. So what does the East Coast have to offer outside of contrived, incestuous national debate? With not enough cash for a Miami-bound flight, a one-night vacation provisions the Jersey boy to Atlantic City, and so it is here that we drive.

For me Atlantic City held no expectation. I can't say that I have ever read any literature about the place. I've never seen any documentary footage or been engaged in much discourse in concern of the town. To me this was a clean slate, an empty canvas, and a free and accepting perception to be crowned or soiled by one night's merit. I'm just along for the ride.

Friday afternoon errands were rolled over to a Monday morning, and loose ends were tenuously tied to a garbled answer phone message. Fuck that shit. I might just be dead after this night of drinking, so I may not even have to call the person back. You're fucked if you think that I'm going to do it this late on a Friday. Responsibilities are dropped for weekend hedonism; phones are left to ring, and incomplete tasks are swept under the carpet. If it works in animated cartoons, then I gamble that it will work for me tonight.

Only *tomorrows* understand consequence; *tonights* are obnoxiously ignorant.

The door is locked and the alarm code set before professional morality can influence me for the better. The logistical operation of the soccer academy can wait a day.

A quick trip home facilitates a rapid shower with just enough time to stuff a morning shirt into a bag and to grab my white loafers. Toothbrush in my back pocket. Six drinking buddies jump into the minivan. Well, in fact, just I jump into the minivan while five others debate the driving duties and squabble for shotgun. I'm on my third beer and holding two more, which excludes my driving responsibility, and my back seat next to the stereo speaker is now warm, so I leave them to arbitrate without me.

In the company of mature professional soccer coaches there is only one way to mediate a fervent dispute of who has priority on seating arrangements. Sudden death rounds of "rock, paper, scissors, shoot" are played out with schoolyard disorder and rule referencing. Rock beats scissors. Aggrieved losers adjust their driving position and adopt backseat settlement. Five CDs are loaded, a bag of chips is opened, and a few beers cracked. Hide the beers at least until the parkway.

"How does a rock beat a pair of scissors, I mean, come on?" Forget about it.

The southbound parkway is a secret shortcut kept secret from none. More cars than have ever been made edge at twenty miles an hour away from metropolitan congestion with contradictory fender-threatening hesitation. Escapism is contorted in the world of facility for quite a few miles as six lost songs and an abandoned bag of chips take with them an optimistic atmosphere before the city skyline is even out of sight. All roads lead to somewhere; all roads lead to this road it would seem.

Persistence and temperance deliver the virtue of the wide open spaces in just less than three hours. In a more reticent community, this time delay could cause problems. In the community that is Atlantic City, I wouldn't be surprised if we still turned up early.

Once liberated of motoring inhibition, the path is free and straight. Small-town Jersey is ignored. Diminishing parkway numbers are the priority now, along with the preservation of time. Speed limits are fractured, as reprimand is just a flirting concern. I'm not even sure if anyone holds a Jersey driver's license. I think it matters little, as two empty crates of beer cans and a shallow vodka bottle litter the foot well, threatening to jam the brake peddle.

Turn left for Atlantic City. Salvation is signposted with omissible efficiency, and we do not have a map to reference. Last-second instinct is believed as two offside wheels camber our egress at the correct intersection, cheating a next junction U-turn, while gratuitously speculating near certain death in a reservation bound accident of lane-veering proportions. Honking horns and road rage are the only evident consequence for aggressive manoeuvring, where perhaps fatality or at least an insurance claim should be palpable.

A shimmering horizon just beyond our view rises with expectation. A few prone postures change, and the discourse raises a smile and a jibe. Billboards replace road signs, and vibrancy trades apathy. The final few level miles grow the floodlit towers of Atlantic City. Vegas's little sister was within touching distance now. And I want to touch her. Casino names and hotel reputations shine bright in the night sky, enticing whomever they wished. Tonight they wished me.

Three cell phone conversations with a hotel concierge made evident that a room in this town might be as difficult to negotiate as the exit turn. Another two phone calls, however, and abodes were found. It's not pretty, but then neither are my. Aesthetics of your hotel room is of little relevance in Atlantic City, facility is a sentiment fully endorsed by all. The bag is jettisoned, and my back pocket toothbrush removed in a matter of cologne-splashing seconds. Three credit card hotel keys are divided evenly between six people, and the door to domestic responsibility is closed for the night. I didn't get a key. I lost to scissors.

A British casino is an upper-class privilege, where membership, invitations, and dress codes are mandatory. In New Jersey, the higher echelons of society are replaced with population. All are welcome to a New Jersey casino, and very few are new. The excessive threshold initiates an overwhelming sensation rush to the casino virgin; the magnitude of everything is incomprehensible. Row after row of revenue-generating slot machines scream for pennies to be inserted just as quickly as they can gobble them up. Whistles and bells and an enormous electricity bill counterfoil attract an endless stream of willing custom like a candy store window can mission school kids to a sugar-rush purchase. Fat people and poor people sit next to obesity and poverty with equal agenda. Roulette tables are wedged to capacity with spectators just itching to trade their exclusion for a piece of the action. The Friday night fervour pushes table prices higher and higher as demand exceeds the excessive supply of agreeable dollars. Chips are gambled and inevitably vanish, and they just keep on coming back for more. Somehow there is an accepting realization that the money is already lost, and so you may as well just keep on playing. This is an intriguing industry. Winning or losing seems of little consequence to the multiple consumer.

A few moments of indulgence are turned at the roulette table; I cash out my sixty dollars at the point of sensibility. I avoid the low gamble machines and search well for the bar. I recline with conversation in a very elegant room that contradicts the clientele that they host. Outclassed Americans adorn plush furniture with inappropriate familiarity. To be so divinely seated suits my taste enough to ignore his perspiration-tarnished shirt and that unacceptable white sports sock and sandal combination over at the corner table. A couple of disproportionate tips keep the drinks lady in favour for as long as I need.

When late hours turn into early hours it's time to increase the tempo a little. The open-door policy of the casino floor procreates this population, but now the time for change and addition has arrived. The vitality of youth and culture draws my requirements to the in-house club, a devilish room of iniquity and obscenity promised behind an obscene and devilish cover charge.

You have to say that nearly naked dancers of nearly perfect perfection are nearly always worth whatever cover charge necessary. Tonight is no exception. Just what type of girl chooses to be a nightclub dancer in Atlantic City? The type of girl that I can't afford to know. Pursuing her with nothing more than my British charm and sixty dollars would be a redefinition of futility to embarrassing standards should I have actually pleaded sobriety and introduced my courtship to the wiggling little angel. I didn't ask, and she didn't have to say no—probably the best for all concerned. I think she knows exactly what she's missing.

Lost opportunities are left to lament as directions change. A comedy fall contest is initiated where the most outrageously feigned ground-reaching stumble is to be judged on the application of forgery. The winner is crowned by the descent that receives the most attention and that intrudes or involves as many innocent bystanders as possible. The potential is absolutely endless. Innocuous stairwells, a tactile dance floor, or an errant beer bottle can all improvise as the catalyst for competition entry. Authentic injury is always unfortunate but often inevitable. Things are getting messy.

Four hours and four hundred dollars meets the early morning sunshine, as tomorrow is as unexpected as it is premature. The ocean view balcony bar rests my weary, but not yet broken body, with friends and faces of limited recognition. The shattered morale of a once-great man leans on the call for last orders, covered in fatigue, red wine, and somehow covered in sand.? The people have gone, the drinks have gone, and finally time has gone.

All I need now is to find one of the only three people in this city who can provide entry to my hotel room and all will be good.

Shotgun not driving home.

I fucking hate scissors.

#9: American TV

There are some things, maybe even many things, that make America the most amazing nation on the face of the planet. I am still trying to work out where TV fits into the hierarchical ranking of most significant U.S. export.

Comedy is a good place to start and situational comedy is an even better place to start. As an avid and wealthy consumer of sit-coms, American TV offers me the perfect pleasure of catching up on back dated episodes of some of the most significant and precise comedy around. At any half hour increment of the day, I can flick a channel of American TV to watch *The Cosby Show*, *Cheers*, *Taxi*, *Frasier*, *The Simpsons*, *Friends*, and the daddy of the lot, *Seinfeld*. Seinfeld is the cutest of all sitcoms and is my favourite American TV available.

British TV is a different animal from its American counterpart, and then again very similar and all at the same time. British TV can only offer the viewer five channels, and out of these five channels perhaps only 3 percent of the material is worth watching. American TV matches up with accurate statistics, where out of five hundred channels, there is still only 3 percent of stuff worth wasting your time with. In America you just have more variety of crap. A thinner spread of the shit. As a reader rather than a viewer, I have to say that finding your latent thirty minutes in five channels is an easier task than finding your *Cosby* in a five hundred option minefield.

Locating a news broadcast on American TV is a different proposition than achieving the equivalent assignment on British TV, and it goes some way towards explaining to me why America is such an autonomous country. I think that it is a world perception (it is certainly a British perception, and it was definitely my perception before arriving here and has been a compounded perception since arriving) that America is a nation interested in only itself, and outside concern really is of no concern at all. I think that being the most significant country in the world you can afford to be and get away with being this conceited. However, I think the difference between America and Britain can be surmised in the detail of news broadcasting.

With just five channels in Britain, we have to be more frugal with our programming. We are not TV affluent enough to afford whole channels specifically assigned to one vertical market. What this means is that every now and again within your mainstream programming you will come across a news broadcast. It's inevitable. You may not be a consumer of news, but while you're waiting for the period drama or for the cooking show or for the football you will inevitably come across some sort of world news. Like it or not, you will subliminally be keeping up with current affairs to at least some degree of recognition. American TV is different. The news will not find you; you have to go and find the news. Everyone knows where it is—it's on channel five hundred and something—but the point is that you actually have to make the effort to keep up. In Britain it just passes over society, and so everyone is a little bit informed. In America you can go a whole lifetime or a whole culture without ever flicking to the correct channel. The American lifetime and culture is then one of total ignorance to anything beyond an American theme. Maybe in Britain we have to be more receptive to world affairs where the American doesn't, but for me the difference is simply the amount of information that manages to seep through to a population.

In Britain we have the BBC. The British Broadcasting Corporation is a government-subsidized enterprise that offers elite programming to patrons for the nominal and annual TV license fee of two hundred and odd pounds sterling. Though heavily financed by the country, the product is often far from impressive and contributes much to the 97 percentile of crap. When investing the nation's money, there seems little room for imagination, innovation, or risk taking. The BBC delivers a lot of regurgitated rubbish that housewives, the family man, old folks, and the weak will accept as adequate return on their investment. Short of an inspirational anomaly, the BBC betrays a TV viewing nation, as far as I can see. Or not see, if you know what I mean. However, the one reprieve that the BBC does offer is a very important one, because the BBC is commercial-free programming. No adverts.

How the American public can let the networks get away with four commercial breaks within a thirty-minute show is well beyond my comprehension. Which corporate think tank or consumer focus group felt that we needed a little breather after the endurance of the opening credits? Even within our highly stressed power-world and our multimedia culture, surely we still command a wide enough attention for six minutes of sit-com viewing without the need to rest a while.

It's not as if the advertisements are any good. Take it from me: we're not interested, we don't want it, we're not buying that shit. And that's where my whole argument fails, because we are buying that shit; we're buying that shit like crazy. It's selling like hotcakes, yet no one has the judgment to actually sell hotcakes: weight loss amnesty tablets, hair growth potions and peachy skin lotions, male enhancement hexes, sexual prowess creams, computer illiteracy DVDs, magazine subscriptions, dental health care plans, genuine diamond jewellery, lifestyle reforming cooking utensils, hotcakes! George Foreman Grills and eagle-embossed two dollar coins that cost more than two dollars. Where other than America can you buy a two-dollar coin for more than two dollars? Exercise equipment that you can use age fifty ... age fifty ... steak knives that can cut through a shoe. Who the fuck is using a steak knife to cut through a shoe? America, tell me; I want to know. Just stop cooking your steaks until they're as tough as a shoe. Buy a George Foreman Grill instead; I hear they're very good. Or steak knives that can cut through a beer can. If you drink less, then you will have fewer beer cans available to experiment with, and your new-found sobriety might decide that you don't need to waste any amount of time cutting cans in half. Try cooking with them.

"Take my highly expensive and corporately advertised tablet along with a revised exercise and diet regime and watch the weight fall off." Save your fifty-nine ninety-nine a month and just get off your fat, TV-watching arse. It's not the tablet that's going to help you; it's the exercise and the diet bit that is going to work. If you go jogging and start eating salads instead of Jimmy Buffs Italian Hotdogs, then you can pop an M&M placebo, and the bubble butt will start to go. It's not the pill; it's the perception. So please stop fuelling the industry and stop calling in within the next twenty minutes. It's a lie and a charade, and you're just duping yourself. With just one month's subscription of this simple pill ... *bullshit*. Don't comply.

The *"call within the next twenty minutes ... "* is absolute hilarity to me. How is it possible that a thirty-piece kitchen knife set of industry quality that cost $600.00 could now possibly retail at $29.99 given the additional overheads of a nationally television advertising campaign. And what happens if you call after twenty-one minutes? Is that it? Is the deal off? Are they really going to turn down my business based on sixty seconds of tardiness? I doubt it.

Pay with a major credit card and get a second product free. Wwwwwwhat? That's a ten million percent reduction in price. America, this just isn't possible. Something has to be sinister here. Quick, find my card. I only have nineteen minutes left to buy. Oh fuck, not enough time to get my fat arse out of the chair. I'd better get the diet pills as well. Hurry up or you'll miss *Seinfeld*.

Don't change your penis; change your wife. There might just be an advertisement for that in six minutes time.

Hang on though, when does the busy British soccer coach actually get time to watch TV? We all thought that you were too busy teaching the soccer elite, not wasting time with television. Very true. Let me explain.

There are a couple of ironies here. Look out for them. The first I will give you for free, and the second I will give you at half price, if you call within the next twenty minutes, that is, and pay with a major credit card. When I was back home in Britain I would only be able to watch two English Premiership football matches on TV over the course of a weekend, because live televised sporting events compromise gate receipts in a country as small as mine. However, being three thousand miles away and with the lost revenue of my stadium entry fee, I am granted by Fox Soccer Channel the televised viewing of six weekend Premiership matches in exchange for what I regard as a nominal and amicable subscription charge. I can watch more English football while in America than I ever could if I actually lived in England.

The only thing is that pretty much every Premiership game is played on a Saturday or a Sunday, which happens to coincide almost inappropriately with my heaviest workdays of the week. Of course, all the American kids play soccer on the weekend. My subscription expenditure now seems futile and redundant, as Manchester United, Everton, or a north London derby is exchanged for a KinderKicker program or a makeup game for my U-12 C team that I couldn't really give a shit about. Work is work, and it pays the bills. It's just that at the minute my biggest bill is my Fox Soccer Channel Premiership subscription payment.

However, New Jersey in late fall and early spring is a meteorological conundrum, and so the annoyance of a rained-out Saturday session can often be a God-given gift to my football viewing benefit. I charade a disappointment and disdain that the American soccer parent would not happily throw their child under the rain clouds to practice soccer skills, claiming that thunderous noise and lightning strikes would not inhibit the attendance at a British soccer school. The simulation is pulled, and they ride home safe and dry, while I ride home quicker, hoping to catch the second half of a six-point relegation battle.

I arrive back to find my housemates dressed head to toe in soccer appendage with the same purpose as myself. Some are head to toe in mud, given their started and discarded coaching sessions. None are happy. The irony of days off and the weather. The electrical storm that has rendered my balls skills program abandoned has also wiped out the dish connection. All I have is static and fuzz and no cable.

Six live Premiership games you can't watch because you're working, and then six live Premiership games you can't watch because it's raining.

I only get days off in the rain.

#10: Order and Law

Residency in New York is a busy existence, which means I most often return home to a garbage-cluttered front room and to an odour that I would rather not investigate further. Housekeeping is an activity best invested in a tomorrow. The reason for my tardiness is clear and known. When school night apathy can't exploit the diversities available in this town, a yellow page is turned to order my pleasure, one of one hundred numbers on finger-smudged file. Twenty dollars and twenty minutes investment will see an amicable ethnic hand-carry a parcel to me, now for my custody, once wombed in puffy red insulation. The smell of cardboard, of bacon, pepperoni, and ethnicity is my pleasure. New York pizza is the definitive product, and the pizza delivery industry is the most sound of business models ever to be conceived. I support the project with vehemence.

I now have a number of pizza pie vendors in this town on speed dial, and I love them for it. Sometimes I don't even have to speak to the guy who answers the phone. A combination of knowing grunts and affirming noises is enough. He knows my order before I do; he's making my requisition before I have even asked. The loaded ethnic is in the car before the phone is down. At times they have even come round on the presumed confidence that I may just want something. And I do. It all makes for good business that some could imitate.

That's their industry. So to my industry. I can spend a lot of my precious moments of time sacrificing my religion of soccer to the spirit of revenue, forever in the pursuit of the yet-to-be-assigned dollar and selling myself that this money should be spent on soccer rather than education, movies, gasoline, or tennis. It may as well go to soccer rather than tennis—that much I can believe in. Integrity sees you honour your obligation, but few would say it ideal in the grand plan that is still with the architect. Blueprint and implement are two different things. Many don't have an architect. Most don't even have a blueprint. At least I have New York.

In the world of seven-day employment, the *public holiday* is chief, governor, president, and captain of everything. A genuine day off. If I had to choose just one, the pizza or the public holiday, it would be a tight call. Fortunately for me, New York provides both. Unfortunately for morality, my Memorial Day vacation is license to forget instead of remember, as I embark on an evening of hedonism and debauchery reaching excessive degrees. With no sunrise obligation, another trip to Atlantic City is conceived. (AC if you're impatient enough to need abbreviation. But don't confuse that with air conditioning, which I did for the first few weeks.) Drive fast and south; follow the signs when mandatory, and we'll sort out the rest when we get there. The required destination is directed with elementary fortune. A satisfactory room is located and paid for: fifty dollars a night; fifty dollars an hour when you return at eleven and have to vacate by noon. Holiday traffic home is as predictable as piss stops and vomit stops. A diner breakfast interrupts many problems: scrambled eggs with cheese, Canadian bacon, sausage, and home fries. A stack on the side and coffee. White toast. There were two more vomit stops after this.

One day away can see many of America's many cultures supported in a short period of time, and all but a few were a pleasing encounter. The next, however, was not. The homeward bound conclusion revealed an inadequate dead bolt splintered from its front door housing with forcefully gained entry. A debilitating recognition of intruders. Tabletops lay vacant where a stolen games console, a half-decent Apple Mac notebook, and a digital camera once resided. You won't get those pictures back. At times like this you can lose a few emotions as well as your property. Security has a contradicting meaning when you feel violated, and confidence and faith vanish as rapidly as your Play Station.

Still, not all is lost. I have friends on my side. The NYPD will flex their impenetrable muscle and squeeze the city crime till mercy is beseeched. In truth it never really quite happened like this. Being a native out-of-towner, the only real frame of reference that I have for the New York police is the illusion fabricated by the media world of television and movies. Starsky and Hutch just used to buy off errant Harlem bar owners instead of doing their job. Cagney and Lacey fought against the oppressive, male-dominated regime inside the precinct rather than fighting crime on the outside. And though not NYPD specific, Chief Wiggum rules the satiric world of the Simpsons with a disappointing accuracy and similarity to his unanimated colleagues.

Our little New York crime occupied three police officers for just under an hour. I felt that there were two too many officers present. These guys could have been better deployed elsewhere—maybe on the streets fighting crime, or maybe pumping gas in Jersey, or maybe something less cerebral than that. I find one incompetent person easier to field than three. The story is a pretty simple one to comprehend. Four of us left for Atlantic City yesterday. Two others left the front door locked this morning at approximately 11:00 AM. The four Atlantic City trippers returned at 7:00 PM to find the door smashed and the stuff gone.

"So you were in the house when the crime took place?"

"It's not Mastermind you dumb fuck. No."

You kind of live in hope that all those exaggerated perceptions and derogatory characterizations that deride much comedy of the police are just misnomers and anomalies of reality, embellished for sordid entertainment. The incompetence of the body empowered with the law enforcement of a given society should never be ridiculed in such evident ways of recognition. However, this is often how the doughnut munching, chili-dog ordering, coffee-break taking, bungling Keystone Cop is portrayed without alteration in many and every media environment. And this is what my guy was like as well. He warranted and perhaps even exceeded every failing example that my prejudice had been prepared for, but optimism desired would never materialize.

We seemed to be being victimized or made to feel that it was our fault. The door wasn't strong enough; the lock was inadequate. Why are you leaving your house unoccupied in half-day increments, inciting criminals and crime? If you have such expensive and sellable items, then of course you are going to be targeted. How is it our fault for living a lifestyle of moderate comfort? I want to live in a life where criminals are the offenders and not me for owning something enviable.

"You live in a bad area, kid. You have to expect that these things are going to happen."

No. Fuck that. You expect this sort of comment from a consoling mother or an empathetic friend; not from the person who is sanctioned and salaried to prevent such an activity. The absolute concession of defeat was unacceptable. I fully understand that there are greater victims in this city than me, and I wouldn't have such an issue if I could see some reverence towards these other crimes being eliminated. I'm just not sure that I do though.

While surveying the crime scene, my officer takes absent amusement in our dartboard and then a talking Rocky doll that would have occupied his time far longer had I not forced an interlude for the progressive benefit of his crime report. His flippant attentions seek out the unpaid parking ticket, pushpin adorned to my notice board awaiting morning consideration. You're not here to interrogate me. Do your fucking job.

I didn't want to prejudice the police, and I didn't want to adhere to the ridicule, but in my example, they totally lived up to expectation, which of course was no expectation at all. At the burger stand and at the coffee counter I invariably see a two hundred pound police officer skirmishing boredom and not crime, their starched and rigid uniform stretched to duress across incompetent shoulders with utility belts riding at nipple height to accommodate obesity. The proud and authoritative look is replaced with a vacant stare. It's enough to promote crime. I would fancy my chances against this bastion of truth over the suburban garden fences, even with someone else's flat-screen TV under my arm.

When all said and done, the crime was reported, the criminals still run free, our stuff has a new owner, and the city remains pretty much unchanged.

On delivery of my pizza, we chat at length about the events of a sad day. Altruistic in empathy, my ethnic comrade asks if I want him to make a few phone calls to his *friends* on this matter. Here we go: he's Italian; he wears a lot of jewellery; he has a big family, most of whom live in Jersey; and he owns a restaurant! Here's the phone. Call whomever the fuck you want.

I am not sure if he had to buy off an errant Harlem bar owner, but something happened.

We got the Play Station back and the laptop. We never saw the camera again.

It's amazing what you can order in this town when the local people know more than the knowledge does.

#11: I Went to the Baseball to Watch the Stadium

There are many institutions in America, and some of the strongest of these institutions reside in New York. Some of these institutions are good and some are bad. That's just my personal perspective mind you, but then some are undeniable. I have traveled this city a little bit. I have been uptown, I have been downtown, and I have been out of town, and what I have come to realize is that all and sundry have an opinion on the New York Yankees. The soccer equivalent back home is Manchester United Football Club, a veritable consumer giant in the sporting world, comparable with your pinstripes on many echelons and none more prevalent than a marketing agreement, negotiated at high boardroom level between the two most saleable commodities that professional sport can find to bridge the cultures of the North Atlantic, North America, Great Britain, Europe, and well beyond.

I struggle not to curse when American childhood innocence fails to recognize that Ryan Giggs is a salient soccer player at one of the finest organized organizations on the planet. It should hurt more that these same kids find his and my native country of Wales a more abstract concept than the world renowned soccer of Manchester United; I take heart in the negligence of third-grade geography teaching for that. But I do fail to condone America's narcissistic attitude towards the triumph of European soccer.

In my short and beautiful time in this city I have learnt many important lessons about this land. One of the most important is to lock your door. Another is that there are plenty of contributors to the American dream, but one stands more proud than most. I have yet to witness a more hereditary American activity than a Yankee baseball game.

We embark on a trip to the Bronx, an unsavoury part of town, dispelling this misnomer with an elegant commuter ferry ride from Jersey. Twenty minutes across the Hudson River dazzles my shaded eyes as shimmering refraction exaggerates the glass-panelled high rise of Manhattan. As if the view alone wasn't impressive enough, you are somehow punished for the privilege of being silenced by such a sight. A New York skyline carries its own enigma without my written contribution. It's worth seeing is all that I will add to the endless documentary.

An errant but far-from-worthless decision was made to board the ferry, as poor advice or poor judgment has sailed our tardiness away from the stadium and to the antithesis of the island for alight'enment at Battery Park. Further away from our destination than at the journey's inception, we now have inevitable choices. A northbound avenue would propel a yellow cab and patrons towards the Bronx, encountering unenviable traffic and the inhibition of lights. A subway trolley can deliver your purpose, but only after many a painful number of stops. Mass transit is not the language of a man in a hurry. I have to say that I have no real issue with an underground system; the London commuter world will find their system abhorrent and irreplaceable in perfect tandem. As an occasional consumer of both cities' facilities I make considered judgment when I declare them enchanting. When time is never a pressing factor, I could spend happy days watching the faces, just contriving chronicles of their chosen motive for today's travel. Just where is this guy going? And why is he going there? I prefer not to ask. Intrigue commands more intriguing if unresolved. There is, however, reticence towards the capriciousness of the subway with a ticking clock as a nemesis. Limited options breed necessity. We jump the tube.

Forty-five minutes—it could have been longer, but I doubt whether it was less—puts us at game time outside the stadium. *The Stadium.* Yankee Stadium. The underground tracks now ride high above the streets, so far out of real estate that no longer does social advantage need to be banished to the deep for financial productivity or efficiency. Elevated tributaries deliver the heart, the life, and the dollars that propagate the Yankee existence. A gentle coast into the station offers a delightful appetizer of the prospect with a diminutive glimpse into the arena through the smallest of gaps; the tiniest invitation only to be instantly retracted. It was quick, but it was my first witness of the pulsing emotion embroiled in the event, and I want in. A million New Yorkers left the train all at once, a mass of anticipation. Every one of them had their archetypal New York accent. They all seemed to be eating bagels and drinking coffee or watching Woody Allen movies; they were all perfectly New York. What they all did have was their pinstripes, and everyone carried their opinions.

The steps from the L train to the street were all prospect and expectation. Maybe the last few were even hope and need. The shadow-speckled sidewalks were littered with chili-dog wrappers, errant fliers for whatever, redundant beer cups all too easily consumed, and the mess that a game-day crowd has the concession to make. We kicked through and presented our tickets at the threshold of Yankee Stadium to a barcode scanner. The entrance was riddled with proficiency as streams of people entered, ridiculing the cast iron mechanical turnstiles that still liberate entry to most British soccer stadiums. The Yankee consumer demands contemporary admission to his game, while the gatekeeper at my hometown soccer team has endured a hundred years of game-day service. His pension can't afford a smile, and he smells vaguely of urine as he hands back your validated ticket stub with laconic ineptitude.

We get seated, accompanied by the aroma of manicured grass, a perfection laid carpet that is an incandescent Kermit green in the evening sun. Everything is faultless. What do you expect? This is The Yankees. Thousands and thousands and then even a few more thousand adoring fans ride high into the night in a horseshoe around home plate. There is simply no escape if it's you up to hit. One man, one bat, as much ability as he can assemble, and countless New York eyes watching you, each with an expectation and forever armed with that opinion which is sometimes all too easily offered. The sight was sensational. Every seat was occupied, and occupied with buoyancy and vigour, with a voice to scream encouragement and where necessary, to scream advice. I find it beautiful when the bus driver, the blue-collar worker, or even the city lawyer deems himself qualified enough to counsel the million-dollar contracted player about his inability to perform his professional occupation. He takes home a million dollars a year because he is very good at baseball. I'm just not sure that he's going to listen to the intricacies of the game delivered by the mailman from the Lower East Side. Shout your piece all the same; you are entitled to.

The game of baseball is played out at an astonishingly slow rhythm. Long periods of waiting are fractured with sporadic moments of more waiting. Infrequently a ballistic projectile is thrown from the mound only to be missed or, even worse, just left by the batter to float by with eventless productivity to the catcher's mitt. A satisfying thud resonates as the catch is completed, and many exasperations accompany from the terrace. "Ooooo … that one was close … he nearly attempted to hit it."

This pantomime continues for a number of throws, and then the batter either walks to first base, or he walks back to his bench. I don't claim to be an expert on baseball, unlike the bus driver sitting two rows back, but I have to say that I did not see too many variations from the procedures that I have highlighted. It all seemed a little bit similar to me. However, there was a comical interlude when one guy hit the ball over the wall and out of the stadium. Good luck to him trying to find that in the morning—he'll be there all day. He must be furious that he lost the ball. His own fault for being too careless, I suppose. Other than that I failed to see how the game officials adjudicated that the Yankees were worthy winners by a score that I can't even remember.

A lot more happens at Yankee Stadium than is hidden behind my written derision for their game and the jest that I poke at baseball. I have to say that I adored every minute of the experience at being part of such a powerful association, and I did understand the respect given to something so important. I spent a lot of my time observing the culture on the faces that were in attendance rather than the on-field spectacle, but then that's just me.

Most had gone to the stadium to watch the baseball; I definitely went to the baseball to watch the stadium. And I feel honoured that I did so.

#12: Apple Smoking

At twenty-eight-and-a-half years old, you like to think that you are eligible enough to make a decision for yourself, certainly a decision that affects the course and the welfare of your own little life.

I've seen movies, and I've seen people; I've walked streets, and I've been in bars; and I would like to think that I am well equipped to form an educated opinion of most things, and within this remit I include cigarettes and the recreation of smoking them. Very well equipped in fact. New York has a different standard and rule from my hometown, in that here the smoking of cigarettes is a banishment confiscated from social pleasure. Smoking is not a vice advised. Well, not allowed is what it isn't. I have talked about this before, and so I don't wish to belabour my vehemence on the subject of apple smoking, but I do want to Midas touch on perhaps a tangent.

I am a subscription member of the smoking fraternity, and I am happy for all and sundry to know this. For me smoking is an emblem or representation of something that I want to be involved with. I like it, and I like people who smoke—not all of them, and I don't necessarily dislike people who don't smoke, it's just that you can often tell a little bit about a person by their habitual failings.

And there it is, the word *failing*. Everyone knows it; society has been well drilled and relentlessly versed that smoking is not a good thing, a bad thing in fact, and now I am even writing it. The reason that I am writing it is that I now stand with a different point of view. With no other motivation than to triumph in a personal gamble I chose to quit smoking. There were a few of the other standard considerations that might have offered minor influence on my decision to relinquish my favourite friend. Health and finance have always carried little concern while I have chosen to smoke; neither have ever provided enough incentive for me to actually flirt with the proximity of quitting, but both ubiquitously remain prevalent. When it comes to jarring a thought of rationalizing the habit, I think that my responsibility to my twelve little honeys carries more weight than most. It would be shameful for my influenced girls to know that their soccer coach was a smoker.

So let's start at the beginning. I am a five-year smoker whose life today is different from that of the person who first chose to adopt the smoking convention—very different. My British lifestyle was one of loose responsibility to others, and so with only my own concern, I was happy to wilt my existence with smoking, as no other would be affected by my choices. Things are not the same today. After living so closely with the responsibility for and accountability to my twelve little honeys, I now have a different judgment. I can no longer look into the eyes of my nine-year-old charges and tell them that smoking is a disadvantage. The hypocrisy is a torment too far, and one that I must address. Parents smoking Christmas cigars and carcinogen-spouting adults are the nemesis of my athletically able players. No longer can I contribute to the world of passive smoking and hold any integrity in the youth development of my soccer players.

And this was my only motivation. There was no other reason to quit than to be faithful to my girl, all twelve of them. On a randomly chosen Sunday night I extinguished my final cigarette and threw fifteen perfectly good ones to the garbage can—a symbolic gesture that pained me. At first the break from the routine and the absence of my companions was strange and wrong, and I hated it. But I didn't break. I stuck with the proposal of quitting. The days of smoking chastity were different but not all together horrible. They were uncomfortable to endure but then far from impossible. In fact, as the days turned into weeks, the issue of not smoking was simply a minor concern rather than an ever-present chore. And so I concluded that giving up the smokes was not that problematic at all, and this dependency was not quite so much a dependency.

At about three weeks into the process, I took time to stop and review my plight. Some inconsistent opinions were starting to be formed. I now considered myself to be a nonsmoker, in fact, a smoker who had quit the habit. Reformed. The conclusion that I came to was that I didn't like being a nonsmoker. I very much preferred being an evident smoker. I now had choices to make. For all the world I wanted to rejoin the ranks of being a smoker once more, only this time my opinions were being formed from a different and new position, a position that I had not been in before. I was not a virgin smoker looking to initiate the habit for the first time with blinkered and shadowed opinion. I was not an abortive nonsmoker who had failed to quit and slipped back into the doldrums of habitual dependency. I was an educated person who had empathy from all points of view who now felt that I wanted to be a smoker. If I wanted to quit, then I could. After all, a month off the scag showed that I was not fighting to stop. But in addition to that, I was not starting to smoke from a blind beginning; I had been here before. The position was that I had all the evidence in front of me and the course of action that I wanted to adopt was to get back on the deal as soon as I could.

Admission to a substance rehabilitation clinic requires enduring a program of twenty-eight days. After twenty-eight days you are physiologically deemed to be rid of your addiction. I don't agree with the twenty-eight-day theory when it comes to being emotionally cured, but a month off the smoke is seen as a period long enough to be compulsively free. And so this was my precedent. In order to truly say that I am choosing to rejoin the realms of being a smoker and not just a bungled quitter, I first had to see out the twenty-eight days of abstention.

From this educated position I assessed the reason why I would want to restart. The most salient reason was that I just didn't feel any positive benefit in my health or in my finances after stopping. I didn't feel stronger; I wasn't running faster; I could jump no higher than before. All right, I was about five dollars a day richer, but I always had enough disposable income to squander or invest on cathartic and pleasing activities, and smoking was pleasing. My argument kind of falls down when the main reason for quitting in the very first place was not to betray or to hypocrite my beautiful twelve little honeys, and that reason was still present. I could do nothing about that. This would always be a torment to me.

What was more important was that I knew in my heart that I never really wanted to stop in the first place. I like being a smoker, and I want to be a smoker. I feel comfortable being a smoker. The fact that I gave them up should display that smoking is not a dependency for me but simply a friend that I want to be around. And everybody likes their friends.

I now have a decision to make. The main reason for giving them up still exists, and I am in a position where I can choose to fall either way: I could go back on the smokes or I could choose not too. Twenty-eight days is the benchmark and I am now at 11:59 PM on day twenty-seven. My decision is just one minute away.

It is not with relief but with intrigue that I light a midnight cigarette. I draw heavily, not to fuel an addiction, but with interest in trying to create one. The familiarity of the tangible acquaintance returns to my fingers and to my lips. The smell initiates the reminiscence of old times, and there is triumph in the return of smoking and drinking at my typewriter. But what is this twist of irony? I extinguish my cigarette about halfway through as I can push and force these pleasures that just do not exist any more. I hated it. I didn't like the taste. The smell was repulsive, and the sensation was sore and sour. I didn't like smoking anymore.

This was a travesty and an injustice. My reason for quitting was never strong enough to quit in the first place. The reason to return was educated and correct. And now I don't have affection for the smoke. I feel betrayed that I have lost an old friend that was very dear to me. I feel like I have thrown a good thing away. I feel that I was hasty with my decisions to attempt quitting in the first instance, and now it seems impossible to return. An old proverb rings very true here, in which you are advised to be careful for what you wish for because the results are not always what you might think.

And now I have misplaced an important part of my culture. I have gained five dollars, but I have lost a friend. Now I have nothing.

That's not quite true. I do have my twelve little honeys. And I do have New York City. But I have to tell you guys, you better be fucking good.

#13: Have a Nice Day

America is the land of service. The service industry is indeed an industry. Unlike any another city that I have been to, and including my own, New York provides the opportunity for the working class American to live a lifetime of minion status.

Maybe the reason for such a vast service industry is that America does have many more outlets that require this type of employee than we do back home. It is fair to say that there are more diners, gas stations, bagel stores, doughnut shops, and coffee vendors in Jersey than the whole of Britain, but I think that there is more to the story than just demand. I think there is a cultural difference.

For instance, tipping is a unique and ubiquitous American entity that does not exist in Britain but pretty much fuels the U.S. industry. New York bars are forever populated with middle-aged staff that can clear a good enough salary to justify essentially patronizing work. Gray hair and birthdays should have seen your maturity advance you along the corporate ladder to directorship status, but I frequently witness that it hasn't. And probably hasn't even been considered. In Britain your barkeeper will be a minimum-wage university student or a degenerate Australian backpacker looking to raise enough cash to get to Paris for New Year. British service will always be sacrificed for the cheapest option available, even if the cheapest option often has a three-month life span followed by dismissal procedures for tardiness or thievery. We couldn't give a shit about service in Britain; we just care about financial efficiency. You can get away with that if you subscribe to the stereotypes of a complaint reticent culture. I don't think that we don't complain; I think that we now just expect derisory service to be the case. Maybe that's the same thing.

I like the American way. I like the fifty-year-old guy with a smile and a jibe. The fifty-year-old guy is breaking his arse to win my dollar-a-drink subsidy because a dollar a drink is how he pays for his kids' shoes, education, and welfare, and he can just about manage it with an application of courteous effort and a quickly accessible cigarette lighter. Who needs a career?

I see it changing though. Chicken vendors, Big Macs and Dunkin' Donuts now opt for the waste-of-time ethnic employee who can hardly understand an order delivered by a native tone. Toothless and lazy blacks work the grill with apathy and a chipped shoulder well below the standard that can justify tipping. The results are weak. But this is where I see the American service industry headed, and I'm just not sure that this course is a good one.

British politicians buy their candidacies on the high-concept promise of education, education, education. What this means is that we have an undivided culture that demands your occupation is one of good salary, earned at a desk or a consultant table, wearing a necktie or a stethoscope. We do not allow a culture where garbage men, manual labourers, or even bar staff are revered as respected contributors to society. The result of this attitude is one of a piss-poor service industry: too many chiefs and nowhere near enough Indians. An educated population is detrimental to itself. There are too many qualified people and not enough jobs, and no one willing to take the garbage out. The American way is to deprive the population of education ... well, perhaps not deprive, but definitely not promote. Though in exchange for a lack of education you have done the chivalrous thing and made sure that an alternative lifestyle is available. Have a nice day.

Less education is a good thing. A society will always need people to get up at five o'clock in the morning to bake bread or clean the streets or do any number of the million tasks that need to be done that no one really wants to do. In Britain we are all too qualified to work in a bar, and that just accentuates the ever-decreasing decline in our service industry. In America no one is qualified enough to not work in a bar.

One of the community projects that the soccer academy offers is to take some of the less blessed kids from a local middle school and provide education through the medium of our soccer coaching. I very much advocate sport as an excellent forum for life skills. It is, however, an unenviable chore when the work schedule has you down for the eighth-grade shift. A more obnoxious and disrespectful bunch of kids could not have been hand-selected for the chaperoned walk from the school to the academy. The fifty-five minute session is unpleasant and exhausting and is the antithesis of a beautiful ninety minutes with my twelve little honeys. The lack of mandatory social decorum combined with the *attitude* merits my assistance redundant within seconds. Fuck you, if can't even speak to me nicely, then I will give up on you before we have even begun. This is not the ideal delivery from a conscientious professional educator, but I feel very strongly that they made the first move. I was there to help them, and they didn't want anything to do with it. Their loss, not mine. I get to see my honeys at 3:30 this afternoon.

I had arrived at the school a few minutes early as always and walked the corridors that were perfectly American. Exhibitions and artwork adorned the institutional-coloured walls as the noise of a boisterous battle against learning seeped under heavy wooden doors, infiltrating the silence of the school hall. I played with my hall pass, and it reminded me of my school back home, but this place was so conventionally American.

The sad thing about the kids is that I could not see any of them breaking the mould to which they had all conformed. I could not see one becoming the doctor, the lawyer, or the company director. I did see a lot of coffee vendors, garbage collectors, and waiters.

As I have mentioned before, the elite soccer kid should come from this gene pool—the inner-city oppression excavates the diamond from the beaches of Brazil, from the favelas of Buenos Aires, and from the streets of Manchester. These are the kids who should have the passion to rise above, and not a single one of them had any passion at all. The contradiction is that the kids who do have the passion are the privileged kids.

It costs thousands of dollars for the soccer kid to play to the highest standard—professional coaching from the age of six is not a cheap project. By the time a player is ten years old, the very best will be taking three travel team training sessions a week, one two-hour academy session a week, and they will be playing a league game and be double carded to perhaps play twice on a Sunday. And there will inevitably be a select team program on top of all that. The intensity is fantastic. And expensive. By the age of ten an elite soccer player will be practicing to the demands of a professional player, and there is no shortfall in the number of takers.

In Britain the road to elite soccer stardom is very tough, and only a few ever make it. Those who do not only have a compromised education to fall back on, and they slip away to our service industry with a repeated story of how a knee ligament grievance robbed them of their contract. In America we are selling a different ticket. If you want to play in the Ivy League, then a very good way to reach expectation is to get good at soccer.

Scholarships are worth more than the cost of an academy program.

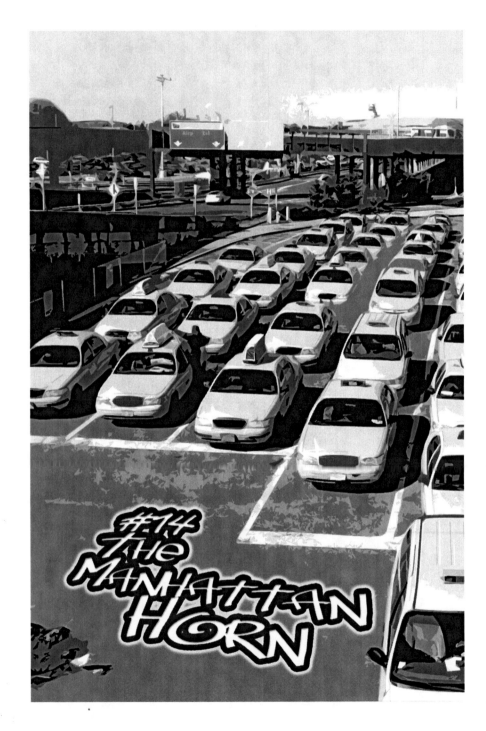

#14: The Manhattan Horn

Driving a motor vehicle in America is a dangerous yet necessary activity if you ever have a need to get anywhere. And more so than any other city in the world, New York presents you the need to get somewhere.

Road rage is a tabloid definition that exists to minimal enterprise on the less sensational Great British infrastructure but reaches some remarkable heights on a Manhattan avenue. Even the country routes of suburban Jersey command enough of a temper for vibrant and excessive use of the motorcar horn. A traffic light sequence at a British intersection will allow the preparatory time of a flashing amber for the preoccupied driver to address and engage the first gear before the commencement of a journey. An American traffic light will skip with little warning from the inertia of a red lit instruction into the free-for-all frenzy of green light liberation, and if you have lingered your attention to a satisfactory radio station search, then now feel clearly warned of the consequences.

The urgency of the New York driver will deem less than half a second ample time with which to react to the green light go, and failure to present intention to oblige will be met with laconic and aggressive retribution. The brevity of horn usage is immediate and often gratuitous in equal measure. It has gotten to the stage where the application of the Manhattan horn is seen as an accessory rather than a necessity; two seconds on your journey delivered by a defensive and courteous driver won't kill you. Driving like a fucker just might though. Yellow cab drivers seem to lean more on the horn than they lean on their driving ability. I don't feel that there is any need other than fulfilling their New York expectation to do so. Fifty-six lane changes from Penn Station to the Village has saved no time at all, and a *bap* on the noise for each adjustment has bought nothing but angst. Not a great exchange if you ask me. Still, who am I to meddle with the way a New York wants to drive his car.

The entry onto or off the exit from a major highway via an American slip road system is a quite wonderful experience that I would not wish on any novice driver. It remains baffling to me how salaried engineers would conceive that motor vehicles speeding up to join a fast-flowing convoy would be put in direct competition for the same piece of thirty-yard tarmac against motor vehicles slowing down to alight. An American slip road provides a direct contradiction of interests that does not need to be gambled at fifty-five miles an hour. Chivalry and courtesy are redundant entities when attempting to join a line of American moving traffic. A British driver will sacrifice their firstborn virgin child to accommodate adjoining traffic; an American driver will kill you in an effort to repel your entry onto their piece of road. As you drive down the ramp, you can see their assistance and altruism being replaced with the reticence of eye contact. Like fuck am I going to let you get one car in front of me, pal. I'm going fifty-five miles an hour, and I have six yards of road remaining before I hit the embankment. Help out! Yield this!

The contradiction to this rather dangerous driving philosophy is more than countered with the American mentality of excessive safety in some situations. It is a conundrum why every car in Jersey has to stop moving when a school child departs from the bus journey home. God forbid, well … legislation forbid that a child be jeopardized on the commuter run. In Britain we go out of our way to remove any measure of safety for the school kids. We encourage children to walk to school in the dark of a winter morning and then without the luxury of parental guardianship or adult road-crossing assistance. Mind you, it is not exactly the elite of American accident prevention that are blessed with an orange vest, a stop lollypop, and the responsibility. At least there is the contribution of the four-way stop sign.

Forgive me if I am too careless with precaution here, but surely a four-way stop sign is a little intense in the way of safety and just about pushing the realms of futile. Stipulation for one line of traffic at a gridiron confluence is sensible, but then also definitively enough. I'm just not sure that dead-end passageway for all comers is helping that much. On you go, sir. No, no, don't wave me on. You go first. No. I sincerely insist, you can go first. Jesus fuck, just go, will you; I've called you on. Right, fuck you, I'm off. Yield this! More angst.

An underused amenity of the American motor vehicle is the indicator. I have never taken a U.S. driving test, but I would like to think that at some point during the examination process there was a little time set aside for the education in the use of this tiny yet very prevalent facility. Without any prior notification, the New York driver appears totally content to administer wild and hostile manoeuvring in blissful ignorance of any restitution or indeed any safety of other road users. In Britain it is a stone-etched commandment that the slightest deviation of any passenger carrier be well considered and evidently defined before such a task conceived. No one gives a fuck in America. Veering lane changes, left-hand turns, and unexplained stoppages are now the problem of the guy behind and really shouldn't restrain your advancement or really shouldn't contaminate your decision to do so.

Aside from the unlawful driving protocol and the neglected pothole maintenance, the Manhattan avenue does have a few redeeming features. Britain is a land of unique motor vehicle manufacturing. Not only do we demand that each and every car is a right-hand drive vehicle due to our left-hand infrastructure, but we also insist on a stick gearshift. The easygoing land of America opted for the automatic staple, and so the benefits concurred. The greatest benefit of all from the automatic automobile is the hands-free liberation. Unlike the constant driving attention that a British car demands, the American highway allows the freedom to drink coffee while you're not indicating. Or drink coffee while you're not letting anybody join from a slip road entry ramp. Or bapping your horn. Or stuck at a four-way stop sign for that matter. Don't move—there's a school child in the next street.

The biggest coffee drinking and driving community that flirts with my little world is that of the housewife soccer moms who deliver my twelve little honeys for Wednesday after-school training. Fleets of Lincoln Navigators and SUVs arrive at the field, and tiny players jump out kissing maternal cheeks, as vast receptacles of Dunkin' Donuts coffee are rested in well-used cup holders for the departing embrace. Ninety minutes of childless time allows for mall shopping, the procurement of Gucci accessories, or a thing with the fling.

My soccer coach vocation sends me happily far and wide around New Jersey as my U-10 travel team does exactly that. They travel. We can journey more than an hour in the endless search for appropriate soccer competition and small-sided tournament play. The family commitment is massive, as whole weekend afternoons are occupied in exchange for sixty minutes of field time. It often takes longer to get there than it does to play the game. To make the time significant and complete, entire families of siblings and relatives trip along and enjoy the spring sunshine with field-side picnics and post game parties.

Regrettably, however, I rarely get to stay, as I race against an endless deadline to make the kickoff of another game for another team at another location. I snatch a doughnut and a medium coffee, cream, and two sugars, and drive the miles, dining from my lap with one eye on the road and the other eye on potential spillages. That's the American way. I never crash, and I never spill. And now I never indicate either. Not enough hands to indicate.

Limited out-of-season vacation time has seen me head back home to Britain. The transition to driving on the other side of the road is a little bit weird, but not altogether impossible. I like the changes and the difference in the driving communities of our transatlantic cultures.

I like being allowed to enter a slip road with courtesy; I like not being beeped at; I like not being shouted at; I like no school bus inhibitions; I like no crossing guards; I like no four-way stop signs; and I like driving on the left. I like the terminology the best though. You say highway, freeway, and expressway, and we just say motorway. We call it a boot, and you call it a trunk—though a trunk is also an elephant's nose, the main body of a tree, and a large case used to transport artefacts for travel. We call it a bonnet, and you call it a hood, which is also an ethnic residential community, so I'm not really sure how any of that works.

On my return to the British driving community I feel comfortable enough to embrace one of the very best driving cultures that I have picked up from being in New York. I stop and grab a cup of coffee to remind myself of just how good it can be to drive in America and bring a little of that back home. The first traffic light turns to green and impetuous horns begin to scream at my stationary verdict. What is this? In the same way that everything American always does, has road rage infiltrated the British lifestyle during my absence? I will be disappointed if it has. Sadly, I feel that the commotion is justified as I have a clear green light and two hands full of coffee and food. But of course, I need at least one hand to shift the gear stick. Nowhere to put my coffee, it's going to spill, and I might even crash.

We don't have automatic cars in Britain and even fewer cars have cup holders. Damn you, drinking and driving.

#15: An Away Day Fixture in New York City

This town has a worldwide reputation that I for one will uphold until the very last minute. I'm just not that sure whether those who come for a cheeky long weekend vacation or an away day fixture in New York City see it the same as me.

New York has undeniably cemented itself as the most salient city location that very few others can touch. London had a go in the sixties, but then the rain got in the way. Paris is a worthy adversary that fancies its chances, but then the French got in the way. And until Paris can lose that whole French thing they ain't going nowhere, baby. Rome, Florence, and Naples have a fair shout at the crown, but they are really only contesting themselves for second place. You have your modern Eastern European contingent of Budapest and Prague, but minus 10 degrees Celsius will soon put a hiatus in most joviality. And then you have your anomaly cities: Sydney is just too far away from anything; Cape Town has the crime; and forget about Rio. Cape Town also has the black thing going on, but you didn't hear that from me.

So New York City looks to its land borders for competition, and there is some fine competition indeed. Philly spawned the Rocky doll—you can kick it you can beat it; it's a Rocky doll. Miami gave birth to Hispanic infiltration. I'm not sure whether that's a good thing or a bad thing. Atlanta's got Coca-Cola. New

Orleans has the Cajun vibe—but then had that storm. Skip Texas. LA, forget about it. San Francisco looks very promising despite the fog and the gays. Seattle has Microsoft and rain clouds galore, enticing nobody with that match-up. Detroit has the major influence of Motown music, but not really since Stevie Wonder hung up his shades. Chicago never really blew it for me—too windy. Denver hasn't been shit since John Elway retired. And Boulder can only crown Mork and Mindy as king and queen.

So, is it by default, or is it by design that New York City takes prize number one on the world stage?

I thought it not even a contest given my own humble perspective, but then a couple of things changed. Well … a couple of things arrived is actually what happened. Homegrown opinion from back in Wales had deemed the New York adventure significant enough to warrant a visit, and so two exiled friendships trip stateside to see exactly what we are missing back in Britain—or not, as the case might well be.

It was my opinion and still remains my opinion that New York is the greatest fascination available to an Earth dweller, but I have to say that a few thoughts were catalyzed after hearing a foreign yet very familiar judgment. When I stop and think about it, the main fountain of propaganda about this city does seem to come from the inside. Most of the informative journals, the radio commentary, and even the musical representation is heavily contaminated by incestuous intention. Simon and Garfunkel, Sinatra, and Woody Allen all kind of came from this town, or a stone's throw away from this town, quite a long stone's throw across the Hudson River if you were Sinatra, but the point remains clear all the same. Are we correct to believe these guys? They all said this town was amazing, and we just believed them. Are we subject to indoctrination or education?

Why the question?

A number of parties have taken the time to visit the abandoned British soccer coach during his New York enterprise. I confess that more came to see the city than came to see the forsaken friend. But then that's the whole story. Everyone migrates to the New York core; everyone takes advantage of my spare room; and everyone comes to see the city, if not to see me. A veritable demographic mix have arrived, done the thing, and then departed with an opinion. Post game correspondence asking for considered rhetoric about this city seem never to reply of a life-changing episode or even supporting the benefit of a cathartic weekend upon the resumption of Monday morning British blues.

How can this be? I was sold on New York before I had even stepped on a Manhattan avenue. I've been here a while now and still my words are unwavering. Yet a mismatch of vacation trippers deems this town as time well spent, but then they also regard New York as perhaps a little promiscuous to claim number one top spot. Have I fallen into the same local quicksand of New York brainwashing, or do we just know a little more than an away day visitor?

Remembering that New York is not my hometown—in fact I have no stronger connection to New York other than this has been my host city for near two years—I will fight the cause for as long as I need to. I am firmly entrenched as a New York advocator, and that won't change for a little while yet.

I ask the Monday morning British opinion for insight into their conclusions and draw a difference in intent, from their opinions and from mine. The museums are shit; it's difficult to get around; the pubs are crap; the queues are long; the girls are rubbish, etc.

And with their answer so comes my answer. What were you queuing for?

In two whole years of New York residency I can safely say that I have done very few of the tourist route attractions or guidebook recommendations. I hate that shit. And there I think lies the difference. I've never been up the Empire State Building and doubt very much whether I ever will. I glanced at the Statue of Liberty, spending more time glancing at the faces of Battery Park recreation. I've had more bridge visits than MOMA visits, and I've always opted to walk rather than to queue at every chance available. This town is not about sights; this town is about streets. Walking and watching is a far better investment of New York time than a straight line of nonsense. Forget the agenda, just keep walking and watching. New York is about doing nothing. It's not about doing something. Walk a bit, stop a bit, and watch a bit. Consume rather than being a consumer. And that's what it's about for me. And that's what it was not about for my visiting delegation. I'm not going to speak for everybody, but that's what it's about for the insider, correct?

For the British soccer coach New York offers a little more than that and a little more than that guidebook, a little more than that reputation, and definitely a little more than that vacation will never see.

The British soccer industry is polluted with nepotism, quality, and competition. And in that order.

In Britain we are essentially a socialist country with lingering socialist ideals. We have complementary national health coverage; we have free education; and we have the social services. We don't pay for medical care unless we want to; we don't pay for education unless we want to; we actually get paid to be unemployed; and so like fuck are we going to spend money for soccer coaching. An American soccer mom will have to find in excess of a thousand dollars a year for her child to play on my select team, and they're under ten, remember. In Britain there just is not the finance available for youth soccer, and so all the responsibility and accountability is pushed onto the professional soccer clubs. What this means for the British soccer industry is that only elite players are catered to, and so only elite soccer coaches are in demand. And so back to my original comment: The British soccer industry is polluted with nepotism, quality, and competition. And in that order.

Ex-professional connection will secure a coaching vacancy just as quickly as you can drop the name of a cup final teammate. Within such a small industry, there are many excellent and well-qualified coaches all fighting for the scraps from a disproportionate number of jobs. So the grassroots soccer coach needs to find a niche. The niche is the affluence of America. And for me, it's New York City.

It's funny, because I just don't see that I have got second best here. Some years ago Britain sent all the convict POHMs to Australia, and you don't hear too many of them complaining about it. I'm not a prisoner of her majesty; I'm definitely here by consent, and I adore it. The reversal of the impossible employment situation back home sits very nicely for me. I coach the most delightful twelve little honeys and wouldn't swap it for anything in the world. I don't coach a professional British soccer team, but then I am fine with my station in youth development that my homeland couldn't provide.

And each day I get to walk the streets of New York. Perhaps one day somebody will notice what this town is about for me.

#16 A Random Thursday Late in November

#16: A Random Thursday Late in November

On a random Thursday late in November my pretty little New York life gets a genuine day off to eat, drink, and smile. Now I give thanks for that. Hang on though; I'm the slaved Samaritan that has to fix the marathon meal for the hungry masses. Give thanks for nothing. However, excellent dessert and coffee conversation wishes to probe a little further and find out just why my new country found the need to gift me a day of reprieve. Excellent dessert or excellent conversation?

Before I dissect and insult the culture and history of another's nation it might just be prudent to have a look around my own glass house first and temper my stone throwing with a little perspective and education. It's not exactly a clear political guidebook that has shaped my own homeland.

The UK is a bizarre and wonderful country that has some strange notions when it comes to politics, and it's a nightmare for the British cartography industry to comprehend. The United Kingdom and Great Britain are essentially the same; they are the same country. Only Britain is a country made up of other smaller independent countries that choose to come together and be a combined entity when there is something positive to gain from doing so. Otherwise Britain is divided into the lesser independent units of England, Ireland, Scotland, and

Wales. I come from Wales. It's the smallest and least powerful country of them all. About three million people—pathetic really. We have our own flag, we have our own language, and we have our own capital city, Cardiff, which is my hometown. However, we are governed by the regency and politics of London, England.

England is a totally separate and autonomous country from Wales. England has its own flag and its own language, and its capital city of London governs the whole thing. Scotland has its own flag, its own language, and it actually has its own bank notes, but it still uses the same currency as the rest of Britain. Edinburgh is Scotland's capital city. Scotland had a referendum a few years back to devolve independence from Britain, but nothing much came from it, and Scotland is still pretty much under British political authority playing out of London.

Ireland is a good one. Ireland splits into further denominations of Northern Ireland and the Republic of Ireland, Ulster and Eire respectively. Ireland's political disparity is a product of religious divide. More years ago than in living memory some Dutch guys had a disagreement over the merits of their particular brand of Christianity and created two factions out of the one common faith. The Catholic and Protestant debate somehow transcended time, geography, and stupidity to manifest itself in Ireland and to be the catalyst of one of the most horrific arguments possible. The political ramifications are that the mainly Protestant Northern Ireland wishes to remain under the guidance of London and maintain British rule and therefore be part of the UK, while the definitively independent, mainly Catholic Republic fights to reclaim its dissenting piece of land via some sickening guerrilla negotiation. Monkey talk.

The Catholic Republic has gold on its tricolor flag, which should never be confused with the Protestant orange that goes back to the Dutch thing. Soccer is a good expression of the religious segregation here. The Dutch national team plays in orange for instance, reverting back to William of Orange and the derivation for the whole religious scrutiny. The Protestant Northern Irish have a modified English flag and play soccer wearing green and blue, the blue signifying a link to Scotland, which is of course under British rule, retaining the ties to the union. The Catholic Republic plays soccer wearing emerald green with gold trim. Not orange trim but gold trim. It's very important that you know the difference.

However, the Irish are a race that liked to travel, and they liked to travel to Britain. This meant that with each metropolitan centre that the Irish propagated, they took their values with them. New York is a good transatlantic example of this—Five Points and the rest. But to remain with the soccer theme for a second, each major British city has a soccer divide, and the origin for the divide is Christianity. It gets diluted the farther south you go, and it gets more irrelevant the more contemporary you go, but the heritage of the divide is still clear. Everton and Liverpool, Protestant and Catholic. Manchester City and Manchester United, Protestant and Catholic. Hearts and Hibernian in Edinburgh, Protestant and Catholic. The word Hibernia means Ireland in Latin. And the most significant example is Glasgow Rangers and Glasgow Celtic, Protestant and Catholic. And a nasty state of affairs it is, too.

We are a politically indecisive country, divided by so many entities including land borders and language, but somehow it all comes together to create perfect harmony. Until you throw in religion. But, I don't want to talk about religion anymore. Sport is the area where we lose most of our international or independent integrity. Each individual country will compete for world soccer recognition as an individual nation, and that distinction will never be blurred, whereas at the Olympics, we will contest the long jump and the javelin throw as a united Great Britain. Ireland will forever remain apart, as the Republic will compete as their own nation while Northern Ireland will join Britain at the Games. The only anomaly is rugby, where Ireland will contest that sport as a unified Ireland, and all of us will play under a British banner, but only on a four-year cycle, and we will never actually compete in Britain.

So, do you get it? One country with two names. One country that is actually five countries but is sometimes only four countries. The two countries have one flag, but then each of the five individual countries also has a flag. Each country has a capital city though neither the UK nor Britain has a capital city. Four of the countries have their own language, and four out of five countries share the same currency. Ireland has its own currency, and Scotland has its own notes. I come from Wales, though I also come from Britain, and I also come from the UK, but I am certainly not English. Easy, yeah?

That is the country that I have come from, and so to America where I now live. In something hundred and something else Christopher Columbus found America. He was Italian, right? And so we get a day off in October. Then a bunch of years later loads of British dudes (they could have been English, two types of Irish, Scottish, or indeed Welsh) arrived in New England at Plymouth Rock armed with the least imaginative place-naming skills possible. Confronted by oppressive times, these Pilgrims called upon Native American hospitality to bail out their malnutrition with a charity of scary-faced pumpkins and tinned sweet corn. And so I get off a random Thursday late in November. In exchange for the food, the Pilgrims showed their gratitude to the natives by reneging on a promise and stealing the land, driving the American Indians into the entrepreneurial world of the billion-dollar hotel and casino industry. The deceitful Pilgrims are left to cultivate the Garden State and return a profit from horticulture and vegetables.

A little farther down the road those Pilgrims who were not boat arrivals but born to the land now consider themselves native. These second generation natives didn't want any more infiltration from outsiders and started to fight them off for their independence—even though they were fighting to stop exactly what they did to the indigenous natives just a few years back. The hypocrisy is sensational. And so I get a day off at the beginning of July. And fireworks for that matter. Oh, we love the fireworks.

Just a snapshot of American history as I see it, though a few pieces of rhetoric might be a little inconsistent. For instance, I don't think that the fireworks are mandatory.

But the fireworks are mandatory … well, they're expected anyway. And this is the swing for me. Independence Day is the biggest day of the year, and the kids love it, and the old folks love it, and the dads love it, and the moms love it, and it's a farce, it's a charade, and it's a lie. The reason and history behind the parade is abhorrent, and no one notices or even cares any more.

Okay, a major rant about the morals of American history, but as you have already stated no one really cares anymore. So where does the soccer analogy come in?

Perhaps not unsurprisingly given the heritage, but the maverick parent of the American soccer kid does sometimes have conceited and exalted expectation of the industry protocol. I have given my time, my consideration, and my effort to each and every little honey on the team, and even though there is definitely a discrepancy with my attentions, I like to think that all get a fair go. However, it hurts all the same when maverick parents betray your honesty, hospitality, and endeavour with dissention and trouble making.

It is a finely tuned gamble to attempt to pursue excellence with an American youth soccer team. As we have read, an American will forgo whatever regulation or obstacle necessary to gain success. As a soccer coach, the cheapest way to gain success is to restrict your team to a subordinate division and watch the American parent's smile as the results roll in. The more adventurous of us like to push the boundaries of excellence a little.

There are few as blind as an American soccer parent.

The parents of my highly achieving, yet not quite excellent, right fullback wish to pull the "superstar player" off the team and drag as much crap and disaster with it. These are potentially detrimental times. It troubles me much why the soccer development, and above all the soccer enjoyment, of a beautiful nine-year-old child should be compromised by the reactive garbling of misinterpreting parents. Just leave the kid stay and play with her friends.

I rank the player as very important and an influence to success, while blinkered paternal opinion ranks her as off-the-chart better than this team. It is a depleting conversation to have to skirt the issue of reality during season evaluations ensuring that honesty equally massages the egos of out-of-control megalomania. The truth remains that the player is good, and I want her to stay, but at what cost? Is he really going to take the kid off the team in the pursuit of a better place to play and perhaps take my genius left-winger with him? This little team means all the world to me, but at the end of the day I like to think that I have some degree of perspective when in concern of nine-year-old girls' soccer. I just can't say the same for the maverick American soccer parent.

I offer my hand in the development of the child as a soccer player, and this is taken with vehement acceptance. Yet under the deceit of the pleasantries there is a plot to destroy everything that I have built, and there will be no remorse or thanks when that is done. The child is nine years old, and she seems to be doing all right. She plays with her buddies, and she plays a lot. She seems to be learning, and I would bet a pumpkin that she's happy.

The kid plays well on a very good team. Give thanks for that.

#17 SNOW WHITE AND THE SEVEN BLACKS

#17: Snow White and the Seven Blacks

The New York weather at the climax of the winter hiatus is a quite beautiful place to be. However, after scraping the footpaths clear of snow for the fifth time in March, it kind of loses a bit of an attraction.

The post-Christmas climate delivers New York a New Year flourish of snow showers that can make even the most urban metropolis the most pristine wonderland. The mansions of the Jersey commuter towns hang fairy tale icicles from fairy tale window shutters, and the impassable roads seem quaint with a clean bath bubble carpet.

Though, it's not all about splendour. I'm sure that a few make a bit of money because of the snow.

State legislation manifests that it is the occupant's responsibility of a residential dwelling to clear the street paths and sidewalks of ground-fallen snow surrounding such a residential dwelling. If each and every person takes care of their tiny little piece of land, then the whole community will be better off for it. Individual responsibility for the greater good of the group equilibrium. Sounds like communism to me. But I like the ideal anyway. We'll call it socialism if that makes it easier.

The concept becomes a little less appealing when a written warning is hand delivered by a disgruntled police officer demanding that the three-foot drifts on our tiny little piece of land be cleared as a matter of urgency; and I'm the only fucker in the house. Suburban homemakers are frequently exploited by DIY warehouse vendors and domestic maintenance stores that consume significant amounts of Saturday afternoons in exchange for the multiple purchasing of futile life-enhancing products. The whole scenario bores me. However, the kick in the bollocks comes when I have been summoned by state law to shift a cubic ton of apathetic ice, and I have invested very few Saturday afternoons buying Home Depot snow shovels. These twenty-five-dollar bad boys can clear a backyard lane in a matter of minutes, given early application to fresh and fluffy powder. I have a consolidated glacier to clear, and all I can find is a Garden State spade at the back of the shed. Times are hard, baby.

Reprieve is never far away, though. The motivational thinking of the modern American entrepreneur is sensational. All you have to do is find a niche, and a market will be formed. Adversity and lethargy are fantastic starting points for a niche. I don't have the tools and even less inclination to clear the snow myself, and yet I have an enforced necessity to do so. And there, my friend, is your market.

A neighbourhood black dude knocks at my door with impeccable timing, flaunting a spanking brand-new bad boy and offering an amicable twenty-dollar service to keep my compliance with the federal authorities. Now, that's a bargain. I watch the second half of the soccer game with the heating cranked up to maximum and with a few cans of beer spilling around the living room floor. He did a piss-poor job, but the police never came back. Winston breaks even after one-and-a-half contracts, even if the work is seasonal and sporadic, though this probably suits his lifestyle, and I laugh in the face of DIY warehouse vendors and domestic maintenance stores at how easy it is to cheat the system. As far as I can see, I'm five bucks up on the arrangement. Until March that is, and then three snowstorms come down in three weeks and now I'm into Winston for another sixty dollars. Don't fuck with the Home Depot strategy—especially when Mother Nature is a shareholder.

The harsh winter elements can be an irritation for a soccer coaching company that trades off having twenty-seven coaches doing three back-to-back ninety-minute sessions on community fields around suburban Jersey commuter towns. The New York winter snow limits everybody to just the one indoor field, and so, as company revenue diminishes, individual profiteering is maximized. Six feet of snow drives the New York soccer industry indoors, and field time is at a deficiency. This means that team training is massively compromised. However, the megalomania of the American soccer parent opens up avenues for a whole new industry to flourish.

The sideline conversation of the American soccer mom has very little to do with soccer; much of it has to do with who has the most modern status symbol. Manhattan-earned dollars of the American soccer dad are eagerly spent on Gucci shades, hip-hop modern soccer mom jeans, accessories, cars, and beach housing. That's just the American way. However, the new status symbol for the American soccer mom is to have a hip-hop soccer kid. And a fantastic hip-hop soccer kid at that. And that's where I come in.

While the oversubscribed soccer fields can't find a vacancy for a twelve-player roster, there are often small pieces of indoor turf available for individual private tuition. And even at the market rate of sixty dollars an hour for my education, there is no shortage of takers after a strong reputation.

I am blessed and cursed with my soccer time in New York. Most of my work revolves around propagating the youth development of a very affluent, mainly Jewish, Jersey commuter town. The combination of neurotic wealth and poor physical attribution makes for an interesting cocktail. While the less religious soccer communities are investing mammoth amounts of time and effort reserving copious quantities of indoor field space to ensure that there is no relapse of game play understanding through the barren winter off-season, the Jewish kids sit with their feet up and their falafels large. Average first touches become obsolete, and the minor semblance of a short-range passing game that was nearly prevalent during the fall season has long since fallen. Division five in the spring is going to be a tough struggle now.

One week before the first game of the season the inevitable call comes through from the team manager suggesting that we start training for next weekend's season opener.

"Jonny, do you have any indoor field time that we can have a practice session before our first game?"

"Mr. Goldburg, you have to understand, the indoor facility is a heated, air-inflated bubble in New Jersey. It's twenty-seven degrees outside, and there are six inches of snow on the ground. We're a desirable amenity during the winter. We have been booked up since the last week in November, and we will be until the first week in April. I have teams coming in at 6:30 in the morning to practice, and they have been doing so for fourteen consecutive weeks. What in the world makes you think that I have a spare bit of field time?"

"Well, do you?"

"Maybe I can jiggle a few things around and get you half a field on Saturday morning."

"Saturday morning isn't great. Do you have anything later on Sunday afternoon?"

And that's the sort of people that I have to deal with—people who are so affluent that they think they don't have to use the system. But, like I say, I am blessed and cursed. The same ignorance, arrogance, and neurosis fuel my individual, private-tuition enterprise. These people become very suspicious of success; I just think that's the nature of successful people, and these are indeed financially successful people. What this means for me is that when a low-ranking player suddenly rises an echelon or two, a few questions are asked as to how this average kid is now a maverick kid. The answer is, of course, individual private tuition. An inspired and motivated player can command a few essential core skills in a very short period of time given the sound application of a strong development curricula and sixty dollars an hour of my personal time. The next question to be asked is, "How does my average kid get to be a maverick kid?"

I now kind of play on the personality of the Manhattan lawyer, on the three-day-a-week dentist, and the company director. I explain that sixty dollars an hour is a rich expense for soccer tuition, and they lap it up with an ignorance, an arrogance, and a neurosis that makes me chuckle. Silly dollars an hour.

"Listen pal, I can afford one hundred dollars an hour if it works."

"No, we'll just stick with sixty, but if you want a chance at making that select team, do you want to go Friday and Saturday?"

The desire to have a status symbol hip-hop soccer kid just accentuates my industry. No complaints from me.

I live a humble existence. I still kind of measure everything in units of what affects my life: $60.00 is 17.1 beers; $60.00 is nearly eleven packets of cigarettes; $60.00 can be seven CDs for the frugal shopper; $60.00 is fifteen Subway foot-longs if you buy on a Sunday or with stamps; $60.00 is a shit load of money based on an hourly rate. It's a lot of money whichever way you look at it, but in my humble opinion, it is an extortionate amount of money when it gets spent on soccer tuition, and it gets spent on a task that a less affluent and less apathetic parent could do for free. Still, I'm not arguing. My adversity and lethargy earned Winston a payday; other people's adversity and lethargy earns me my payday. Affluence and apathy are good things for me. That's my entrepreneurial market niche.

I had one such unknown soccer mom call me wishing to buy my services at the premium rate and, of course, I obliged. I told her that I could work with her son on Saturday from 10:00 AM till a little after 11:00 AM. She requested that I do it Thursday morning. I questioned why such urgency. And she replied that he had a game on Thursday evening. For me, this exactly explains the mentality of the people involved here: one hour of soccer tuition does not take a makeweight player and turn them into Pele at a dollar-a-minute investment. Soccer is a lifetime education that takes application in the pursuit of excellence, with the knowledge that perfection is unattainable. She still paid the sixty dollars; I still took the sixty dollars. I wonder if the kid won his Thursday lights game.

It's hard to explain how this weird soccer community works. Maybe it's just one of those things that you have to kind of see for yourself. I find endless intrigue in the Jewish Jersey commuter town soccer club that I spend much of my time working with; the people are so foreign from my values that it just makes me laugh.

At the conclusion of an inevitable defeat to one of the more ethnic-influenced teams that the league schedule had paired my pointless U-8 girls, division six B team to play, an ignorant, arrogant, and neurotic soccer mom called me aside. She asked whether it was within league regulations that the opposition could field a team composite of all black players. I even think that she wrote a letter to the head office contesting the result after an African American had scored winning goals against our all-white, all-Jewish, and all-crap soccer team. The result still stood.

My housemates return and congratulate me on the snow clearing. "Did you have to use the spade?"

"Yeah. And he only charged me twenty dollars."

#18: iPod or a God?

This is my second New York Christmas, and now that I have learned a little more about my host city, I have to say that I enjoyed this one very much more than the last one.

In Britain Christmas is not really about religion ... well, it's not about the same religion as it is in America. Christmas in Britain is all about the very different religion of soccer. Over the festive period, the English Premier League filters the naughty teams from the nice teams with the most intensive program of fixtures that the season can offer. Five games and fifteen available points will all but banish the basement teams to doom and see only the strongest teams toboggan away out of sight. A game every three days delights a whole nation and boosts the gate receipts with Boxing Day and New Year's Day pleasure. Christmas in Britain is now undeniably about the tradition of soccer, and you won't find me complaining about that.

Christmas in New York is a little bit different though. Christmas in America is still very much cemented with religious foundation, as indeed, this is the true reason for the holy day holiday in the first place. I do see it changing, though. Religion means nothing to us back home, as gods have been shelved for soccer players, and victories are worshiped inside a stadium and not at a temple or a shrine. I like the exchange very much and hope that it takes to such a strong effect over here.

In Britain, Christianity is still pertinent, but only to a few. The church now just has merit to the old, to the lonely, and to the weak. Communities of pensioners bake biscuits and see friends on Sunday mornings, and this provides stability and familiarity to vacant lives. The soiled integrity of the clergy has little respect from an educated population, and as the relevance of the industry decreases, so does its power and its following. Religion has no worth in Britain any more, and as each generation dies, so the decline persists. The legacy of religion in Britain will soon just be a collection of fine architecture and really nothing more than that.

There are still religious undertones to a British Christmas, but the true reasons are skirted over pretty quickly, and now I see the same happening to America, even with your stronger sentiment to faith. I see the odd nativity scene shining incandescent on a neighbour's rooftop, but it's a bunch of bullshit, really. I see Jesus marginalized, as gross profits and revenue remove the religion from Christmas with the vehemence that soccer and shopping has already done so in Britain. Religion still commands a greater percentage of interest in New York than it does in Britain, but it is being detached. And Christmas is a very clear definition of that.

On Christmas morning I didn't go to church, but I trip to see my American family and dine on a champagne breakfast on the most religious morning of them all.

As I step inside the house I am met with the gleeful smiles of my little sisters grasping iPods and Von Dutch T-shirts. Baby Jesus was nowhere. Uncle Leo was around, though. Uncle Leo took me through the intricacies of spread betting on U.S. college football, and we chinked a champagne glass for the eighty dollars that he grifted in yesterday. It is a vastly unknown page in the Bible, but if I had read the good word a little more closely, I would have seen that Gambles, chapter 12, verse 8 of the Old Testament does indeed explain the Christian value of college football spread betting. Check it out. I also missed the act in the nativity scene where Mary and Joseph pulled a cracker at a turkey dinner. The kids pulled my cracker, and I was offered a purple paper crown. I guess that's the three kings bit coming in there. However, I don't recall the three kings giving baby Jesus a crappy yo-yo made in China that doesn't really work properly, or a fake moustache that kind of hurts your face, or a tiny tilty toy where you have to get three silver ball bearings into three slightly undersized holes. Did you ever get a paratrooper guy with a cellophane chute? I did. And it didn't work then, either. And I definitely don't recall the three kings telling very poor quality jokes printed by a fortune cookie company. "Here you go, Virgin Mary, what do you call a dinosaur with one eye?" Hang on, you can't have a Christian representation meddling with dinosaurs—the whole dinosaur evolution Darwinism thing kind of ruins the whole Jesus Christian creationism thing, and yet we now have a dinosaur joke inside a Christmas cracker. What the fuck is all that about? At least do some research.

Where should I put my Christmas gifts? Put them underneath that Scandinavian evergreen tree that wouldn't last two minutes in Bethlehem. Okay.

The biblical links get more and more diluted as tradition takes over symbolism, and I'm fine with that. I like the paper crown and the gift giving. I like the fact that I was invited into another's home in the same way that Mary, Joseph, and the pending family were invited into the inn. But surely we are now just about a holiday and not a religious event. The shepherds didn't get four days off work and queue up in Bottle King for thirty-five minutes, but that's where we're at. Even America is all about the most capitalist of worlds reaching the strongest bottom line, so take the religious connotations out, and let's just have a holiday.

I do hate religion with a passion, and I feel very comfortable poking satirical fun at such an entity, but religion has such a dangerous undercurrent. Okay, nativity scenes, baby Jesus, village jumble sales, and the irrelevant community finding a common crutch to lean upon are all pretty harmless. But I found it most pertinent when a neighbour of contradicting faith made a morning visit to the Christmas Day breakfast. New York is of course a veritable melting pot of culture, and intertwined seamlessly into the culture is the very much more prominent religious divide. Perhaps not divide, but definitely difference.

It was a genuinely sincere couch that saw the Christian communities and the Jewish communities sitting side-by-side as friends and neighbours sharing time and sharing champagne and sharing the day. Christmas Day.

The American Jewish community and the American Christian community live in complete harmony in New York. Of course they do. If the Jews and the Christians can't live in New York together, then you're fucked in every other city in the world. The point is that even under this most hospitable and amicable scenario, there was still time for a contentious debate, and the focus of the debate was religion. It was a friendly crowd, and nothing more than an eyebrow got raised, but the catalyst was as strong as ever. The Jews entered the room with cheers of happy holidays, and the Christians retorted with a very Merry Christmas, and that was the whole discussion.

The major conglomerate department stores of Fifth Avenue wish to take your dollar bill in exchange for a child's Christmas gift, but they won't find the courtesy to wish you a Christian greeting, instead opting for a multi-religion gesture.

How dare the department store or the neighbour dodge the reason for the sale or for the visit with vague referencing? Specifically, this is a Christian festival, and so all should acknowledge the Christian involvement, be that a department store, a Jew, or indeed another. Christmas definitely is a Christian thing and definitely not a multi-religious vacation. It definitely has to be a Merry Christmas and definitely not a Happy Holiday.

The debate continued without my interference for a couple more drinks, and frustrations started to show on a few reddening checks. "So what do you have then, a Han kah Clause, a Yom Kip' Clause or something?" Even though I landed strongly on the side of Jesus in this particular conundrum, I have to say that I find all religion abhorrent. I find it okay that people feel the need to use religion to gift a child or to sound politically correct over the usage of the word holiday. I find it okay that people use this community to feel accepted, to feel social, or to bridge a vacancy. I feel okay that religion provides a nice room in which to get married or to provide closure to the departing. But religion is not a panacea. Religion is not even true.

And it's the truth bit that troubles me the most. The fighting that religion undoubtedly causes probably does trouble me the most, and how that was signified in a rather mild Christmas morning debate. And New York, above all cities, surely recognizes the devastation that religion can manifest, so much so that I don't feel comfortable talking about that even if I wanted to. But I don't want to—not in this town.

Religion provides this false ticket to something so intangible that the subscription rate baffles me. How do so many lives pay reverence to an entity that returns nothing? It's a lie, it's a charade, and the power is disproportionate.

As I have said, my religion is soccer, and at each and every vigil I am given a conclusion on what I worship. I might win, I might draw, and I might lose, but I definitely get a deliverance. I definitely get a conclusion. I may not like it, I might not have wanted it, but I definitely get a return for my faith.

For me religion is ethereal. It doesn't provide a solution; religion is no answer. Soccer may not be a perfect assurance, but at least you know what you get. And Christmas is a good day to recognize that. Especially as we're at home to Man City tomorrow.

#19: Nice Mango

New York City offers the most wonderful range of culture, the most wonderful range of colour, creed, religion, and opinion. The selection is sensational. I've been mugged five times in this city, and each time by a different race. A Korean last night—fifty-five dollars and my Metro card. I can't think of a better town for the United Nations to set up camp.

Even with the very strict contemporary Muslim expulsion, there is still room for a number of religions to take a home in New York City. In addition to the main staples of Christianity and, of course, the Jews, you have a few of the more Eastern and fashionable modern religions coming through to stake a justified claim. Buddhism, Hinduism, Passivism, nothingism, yogaism, soccerism are all eating a slice of the demographic pie chart, and New York City will host them all. I'm not a big religion fanatic, but you won't find me complaining about the range; the variety is very refreshing.

The New York City demographic stretches to even greater vertical tangents, given the migration from the four corners of the earth. The earth is a three-dimensional entity, so it would have to be eight corners if anything, and considering that the earth is spherical, that's a bullshit comment anyway. The collection of New York out-of-towners is an absolute miracle to me and makes for the most enchanting time spent in this city. I just love the diversification.

Early Sunday morning soccer games can see me commence a lengthy car jour- ney at the very break of day for a South Jersey away match rendezvous. After the procurement of coffee, I slide unnoticed through the ghetto streets looking for the parkway entry ramp, concealing my toll money out of criminal view. At a random, an unadvertised street corner, usually the focal point of a supermarket or something like that, a crowd of literally one hundred Mexicans wait for a pickup truck to arrive. Upon its arrival, two ethnics get in after brief negotiation, and literally ninety-eight Mexicans wait for another pickup truck. I have yet to see any publicity or organization of this enterprise; it has simply just evolved. But at casual street corners the American dream offers hoards of workers the opportunity for cash-in-hand manual labour. If you have a construction business, and you need two or more chippies off the books for a day of graft, then drive by and select your man. There's no ticket machine, and there's no dental plan. The venture just progressed, and the venture just works. I suppose it must be better than being in Mexico. The results are evident.

The Manhattan black is a funny race. My favourite black is the indiscriminate singing bicyclist who rides against the flow of imposing and threatening road traffic without purpose or without any care or attention. They can't be couriers because they aren't carrying anything. I know what they aren't, but explain what they are is a difficult thing. I find it hard to understand how such a directionless activity can provide a living; I just don't see what these guys are doing for money or where the payday is. I find it harder to understand how a Manhattan black can even own a bicycle in the first place. They must have pinched it. There is absolutely no other conclusion that I can come too. No, don't even try to enlighten me. I've thought about it, and no other option is valid. The bicycle is stolen. Must be.

My second favourite Manhattan black is the brown parcel trolley pusher. At every road crossing, some black dude with a trolley of whatever mingles with the pedestrians as a cigarette hangs from his lips. Where these guys are going, nobody knows. What these guys are carrying, nobody asks, but they're there. They're everywhere.

In Britain the true stereotype is that corner shops are honoured by Hindu purveyors—some are Pakistani, some are Indian—but all are watching Bollywood movies on an unlicensed seventies black and white TV with a grandparent and a number of small children. In America the Pakistani has found a similar vocation, but in Manhattan he has competition from the Korean. Street-corner fruit vendors and the utility product market have been infiltrated by a Southeast Asian monopoly. The ethnic competition price war makes for happy times if you are a recreational mango buyer.

Chinatown is a veritable assortment of similarity. One poorly maintained fish merchant should not really be strong enough to promote lingering business; yet, how this concept managed to promote a whole city district is about as far out of my comprehension as is possible to conceive. There would have to be the most bizarre combination of implausible events that would see me purchase any food item from one of these guys. I'm no food ponce; I'll slum it with anybody, but like fuck am I going to take home a darn of salmon from any Chinatown Chinaman.

Little Italy is a cute couple of minutes though. The side street Trattoria is a nice little reminder of European heritage. It is hard not to imagine that some money laundering isn't being counted out the back or that someone's eye isn't being popped out of someone's head. Maybe it's just a vandalized parking meter being hammered for quarters, or maybe it's the next Idlewild heist. Whatever it is, it's definitely going on behind that door, and my linguini tastes a little richer because of it.

The Japanese walk the streets with their ceramic child on a piece of string, taking digital photos and generally just getting in the way. The Irish populate the Irish bars—the Irish bars that they don't already work in that is. The Russians and the Portuguese form soccer teams that argue more than they pass, and they foul more than they play. There was absolutely no need to punch him in the face; he plays on your team, for fuck's sake. And somehow the Spanish ended up in the franchise coffee vending service industry or the telesales trade despite not having any discernable command of the language. New York has it all. Whatever you want, we got it.

And the ethnicity that flirts with my little life the most is the ex-pat soccer coach.

The soccer industry in America is an excellent foundation stepping-stone for the British soccer lad who just can't find the work at this level back home. Thousands after thousands of British soccer boys land stateside for a multitude of reasons. Some are wasting time after or even before a university adventure. Some come to try their hand at being full-time and big-time coaches, and everyone else just kind of finds their level at some point in between. What this does mean is that many tribes from Britain crop up all over New York. I flew eight hours and three thousand miles to get here, and now I live in a madhouse of people who all come from a bus journey away from my hometown.

The twenty-something British soccer boy with recently severed apron strings who is now residing in America is a wonderful thing. The enterprise and education for the individual is spectacular. Living in the same house as the consequences, however, can be distressing. It baffles me much how a human can get raised to the age of twenty-three and still remain devoid of acceptable sensibility. Heritage has a lot to play in this. The percentile of social integrity that these people fall into also has a lot to answer for. Stupidity is prevalent, and the addition of heavy drinking completes the potion of a disastrous human.

And then there's the Irish. Lazy fucking idiots. I hate the fucking Irish. I don't wish to stereotype or nothing, but I hate the fucking Irish.

"Jonny, do you have the number there for the refuse department?"

"Why is that?"

"I think I threw away my green card application inside of a Subway wrapper and now the garbage has gone."

"Have you checked in the sofa cushions like last time?"

"That I have."

"And by the way, can I take tomorrow off to go home for my sister's wedding?"

The Glasgow Scottish are a hotbed of soccer enthusiasts, and many wide-eyed freaks with weird accents come to us from such an origin. When diluted from homeland familiarity, their foolishness appears boundless. I can only conclude that acceptance to their Scottish society is welcomed by equal stupidity, and judging by the conveyer belt of ineptitude, my assumption remains with solid foundation. I have seen more Scottish people slip from rooftop perches enduring hospitalization and medical treatment after failed housebreaking episodes due to forgotten, lost, and never-replaced front door keys, than any other gene pool. It costs a two dollar expense to get a key cut, and only the most mild and timid expenditure of remembrance or brain capacity to be a key holder when leaving a property. But somehow, nineteen stitches and an X-ray invoice in excess of a grand seem to be the chosen option of residential entry each and every time. Remember your keys and forget the travesty. Not if you're Scottish.

The English divide into the Northern and the Southern, and a tasty little debate it is as well—unless you come from a standpoint of being Welsh, in which case both and all English are useless. Drinking and driving is the given pastime of the English soccer boy, and a more stupid outlook would be difficult to conceive. Monday morning management assessment of the staff's weekend embroidery will usually consist of having to appease small-town Jersey police offers with regaled explanation of why company vehicles have been left abandoned and distressed in the middle of main street thoroughfares with a grossly misaligned off-side wheel that wasn't misaligned by a pothole at all. You deceitful, drunken, English bastards.

And if you wanted to take the bins out every now and again that would be nice. Or wash a dish or two. Or tape the football upon a request to do so. Or write a phone message on the board.

Before I left Wales for New York it was mentioned to me that I should tap into a few organizations such as the Welsh in New York group and find some familiarity and security. This is bullshit. I didn't come to New York to find Welsh people. I can find Welsh people in Wales; I know loads of Welsh people in Wales. I came to New York to see something that we just don't get in Wales: We don't get change; we don't get diversity. Very little is different in Wales.

"Shamus, is this your holiday request form wedged in between the sofa cushions next to your green card application?"
"So it is. Do I get the holiday granted?"
"I don't think it matters anymore. I've just found your passport in the bottom of the washing machine."

#20: He's Poped His Clogs

While sipping coffee and eating my supper at the nearby diner, the all-American waitress wasted about ten minutes of my life regaling me with her pope story. I have to say that she kind of ruined my ice cream dessert because of it. In 1979, or something like that—I wasn't listening too intently—the pope visited Newark, and she had ridden a bicycle to see him. It wasn't a great story. She cried in '79, and she cried yesterday. He's poped his clogs.

I have talked many times before about religion and how the idea really doesn't sit that easy with me. In fact, I am now an active opponent of religion. Maybe that topic is a different piece of work for a different and more sensitive day. The reason that I write so much about religion now is that I find so much intrigue and interest in the concept, and yet the concept has only really become an influence on my life since I arrived in New York. Don't get me wrong here; religion is not influencing me, but rather influencing the life around me, and I return much enjoyment from that. We have religion in Britain, of course we do, even in Wales, but nobody really gives a shit about it anymore. It was only when I stepped foot in New York that I properly began to understand what it was like for a community to be besotted by God, and then besotted with all the other crap that comes along with it. Yesterday the pope died, and a whole new world of commentary came flooding my way.

First, the pope didn't die; he must have been killed, correct? If God *giveth life* and then he *taketh it away*, or whatever the correct copy might be, then by definition as a believer, God killed the pope. What's all that about? That's a nice end-of-term bonus for a lifetime of commitment and devotion. Cheers, boss. Nice gesture. I appreciate it. Fuck that shit.

April 2nd. Deceased. There's a lot of potential there with that date. It would have been a class gag if he had come out a few days later, resurrected, blagging an April Fool's comedy skit. Ha-ha … I'm not dead at all. I've just been faking imminent death for about fifty years. The pope was about the most frail looking human in the history of frail looking humans. He very much had that Yoda thing going on. I thought he actually might have sipped from the Holy Grail, given the longevity of this *imminent death*. Immortality. Not even for the pope. So what fucking chance has anyone else got? Don't waste your Sunday, people. It's all a charade. Don't waste your sundae.

I find the Catholic religion to be abhorrent and obnoxious. The oppression given by something that was supposed to be a salvation is just so incorrect to me. Families are demanded to give the church copious amounts of money instead of feeding the family—and massive families at that. How intolerable is it to abolish contraception and then to abolish abortion. You end up with six-kid families that can't get clothed adequately because the clergy has robbed all the fucking money for a gold embossed plinth or a Rio de Janeiro statue to sit on the acre of rich and consumable land out front. And after all of that, women's liberation is a concept about as ancient as good old Mr. Christ himself. I'm not even sure if women are allowed inside a Catholic church yet; they definitely can't work there. Unless they're working that is. Clean something up if you want, but like fuck can you be in charge. I've changed my mind. Can I get a divorce from all this shit? Mmmmm … don't think so.

The diner waitress looked long into the distance as her recollection jarred a thought of remembrance in her faith. "I cried when I saw him." What the fuck are you on about, you stupid bint. You cried when you saw the pope in Newark. He's not Jesus, for fuck's sake. You do understand that? The televised news broadcast displayed vigil groups mourning his passing, and the sadness was embarrassing. I didn't get it. I couldn't understand. This dude was not Jesus; he was some chancer from Poland. He was born in Warsaw in 1920 or something; he's not from Bethlehem two thousand years ago. Two thousand and five years ago, actually. He's just a guy. He's not Jesus. Can any fucker hear me? Go home and worry about something important. But can I get a slice of cheesecake before you go please, miss.

I mean, what do we need a pope for anyway? I can tell you for a fact where all the money goes. It goes on his razzmatazz lifestyle. Check out his gig. He gets a house, a proper crib in the nice part of Italy. None of your shit. Not exactly a barn in the Middle East, if you know what I mean. That's a major perk of the job. His air mile coupons must be out of control—trip anywhere you want. He even came to Wales once, I understand. I didn't go. I didn't cry. "Where d'you want to go today, Pope?" "Fuck it, man, let's check out America. I hear they're mad for it over there. Should be a sweet gig." I guarantee he's not dipping into his own pocket for the taxi ride from LaGuardia. He doesn't even have pockets in that gown.

He gets a clothes allowance. Grossly underused if you ask me, though he does have an amazing range of hats. Again, not really maximizing the budget there; but trying hard to funk it up with the hip new Catholic kids all the same. Keep trying, pope. You haven't hit it yet though. A proper pimped up ride. *A proper poped up ride.* I have yet to see an identical vehicle at the Ford dealership. That motor doesn't come cheap. And who paid for it? Correct. Not the pope. Some six-kid Irish family with a tired mother. And on top of all that, he must be on a salary. A pretty good salary, I bet. Well, the pope has to have some flash money, right? He has to pay for the harem of Vatican bitches, Asian nymphs, school children, and faggots that he flies in to the Newark Hilton hot tub spa. I bet he wears that hat while he's being soaped up. I would. Wouldn't you? Why else would you have a hat like that? For no other purpose.

And then I started to think about what the pope actually does to deserve such a prime lifestyle. I looked at the diner waitress, a conformed devotee, and I wonder after the project. He flies into Newark in 1979 or wherever for that matter, on the expense account—just swipe it on the company plastic. He parks up the sweet ride, and Yoda's up to the gold-embossed plinth.

"Hey, everybody, how you going? Peace out, Newark." And everybody, including my diner waitress, gives a massive and in unison cheer.

"Yeah, pope it up, baby."

"Hey, Newark, you guys should believe in Jesus."

"We already do. That's why we've all come here."

"Excellent. Well, you guys should just carry on believing in Dr. J."

"We already intend to."

So what was the point of all that?

There was no point. He's not Jesus. He never was. He's never going to be. I don't know why you went to Newark in 1979 to see a guy from Poland in a hat. I don't know why you cried. I don't know why you're crying now. He's just an old man wearing an outfit. And waving. I just don't understand. And he's a little bit crap on the waving if you ask me. I've seen way better wavers in my time.

The king is dead. Long live the king. What do we learn from this? We learn that nothing ever stops. As soon as one falls off the top, a new one joins from the bottom. Catholicism has a problem to resolve now, though. Whereas the previous four hundred years of Popedom was covered by the last guy, you now need a new guy to step in and squander the next four hundred years of idealism and ignorance. That's a tough ask. "Hey, guys, how you going? Yeah, I'm the new pope. It's my first day. Can you show me where the coffee machine is, please?"

I think that they should spice it up a little with the new pope. I think we're ready, I really do. We could push the boundaries a little with the new pope this time round. He needs to be more modern. We could go for a girl pope. A popess. That would work for me. A glamour model or something like that. What about an Asian? A non-Hindu Asian, of course. Pope Mohamed Ahmed III. Probably the first actually. No. Okay. Latino? Mmmmm ... okay, maybe not. A funky gay pope? That would work, wouldn't it? A gay and lesbian pope with a rainbow ribbon car sticker on the pope mobile. What about a black? A proper fried chicken, chip on the shoulder, baggy white T-shirt African American? That would be brilliant. Fuck the miter; Yankees cap on backward. Cell phone instead of a scepter. Bad language. Undecipherable language. A jive pope. "Hey, dawg, fuck that bitch. You want to buy some powder? Jesus is a top cat, baby." A black pope. That would mix it up a bit for sure. Ned Flanders and Tupac combined. TuFlanders. NedPac. Biggie Pope.

So how do you choose a pope? Four hundred years ago the Vatican had rules and regulations that kind of worked for them back then. Times change though. Things need to be different now. The consumer demands it, and the marketing men should milk it. *Pope Idol.* It has to happen. Reality TV. Ten candidate popes living in the same house for a six-week period without communication to the outside world. I'll fucking pay for the cameras. I want to see that. Vote off a pope each night. To register your vote, dial 1-800-POPE-OFF. You can pope off. Pope that shit. Pope this. "You have no pope presence at all." There's just too much potential here. Too much popetential.

Religion remains absolute hilarity to me. I just continue to find so much pleasure in something so weak. I feel God blessed to live in New York and learn so much about this way of life. And that has to be an apparent contradiction. I worship this town.

#21: Half Team Oranges

My twelve little honeys are two one down in the final game of the tournament. It's halftime. One mothering intention has provided a Tupperware container crammed full of orange wedges. Where the fuck d'you get oranges from?

The New York street is a barren road when in chase of a humble piece of fruit. I think the British side street is a far easier place to locate a banana for the bus journey home or to pick up an apple for the ultimate fast-food serving. New York radio has taken to promoting the veritable benefits of fruit through some rather weak public information advertisements; I can't help but think that they have the strategy all wrong. We already know about fruit. We know what fruit is; just fucking tell us where to get it from. Falafels, doughnuts, pretzels, a Turkish kebab, a hot dog no relish, and a pizza slice are very easy to come across. Some dude will wheel a trolley past you if you just stand still for long enough. But where, my chubby little city, is your green grocer? Does New York not vend a strawberry any more? The Big Apple. I'll be happy with a couple of small ones if you want.

I'm very old school when it comes to fruit. I have to say that I'm not a big fan of the wannabe fruit. I do feel that all of your fruit bases are adequately covered with an apple, an orange, and a banana. I will put a strawberry into that grouping, if I'm asked, that is; you do have to have a berry in there somewhere though. And I give a little bit of credence to the lemon, but a lemon is merely a luxury fruit and far from a staple. You have your big four, and they are pertinently clear and well defined.

The merits of fruit were once very simple. Bananas were once a very minimal snack item with the benefits of its own natural packaging. And you do have the added comedic hilarity of sidewalk discarded banana skins. Though I am wary of people who eat brown bananas, and so I should be. An apple a day would put medical physicians out of work, but an apple would also fit rather nicely into a school child's lunch pack. They would get bruised on a drinks carton every now and again, but hey, we can deal with that. And there is entertainment, fascination, and a challenge to peel an apple in a oner—never as easy as it looks. Oranges were fun if you could just get into the bastards. Only old people and mothers can tackle the endurance of an orange, and even then they require a sharp implement or a thumbnail. And even though a strawberry was very much a delicacy fruit, they were very much popular. And there you have it: the big four. You don't need any more fruit than that.

But then came more fruits, and with this shift so began the increase to the market share. Mangos and kumquats were arriving. Fuck off. We got fruits already. We've got apples, oranges, bananas, and strawberries. We don't need any more. Go off and find something else to do. Be a martial art or something. There's loads of room over there.

In the late eighties and early nineties fruit started to redefine their career path. Lemons began to push their way into the washing up liquid market and the others into the male shower gel arena. Then, from absolutely nowhere, you had pointless and rubbish chancers trading in the same revenue streams. Kiwi fruit and a lime. We don't need you. I'm not at all sure that sanitary products need you either. It's a bit of a boast to attempt to fracture the soap market before you have even established yourself as a mainstay, mainstream fruit. I suppose that's just aggressive modern produce for you.

I always found the cherry as an anomaly, punching well above its weight. Cherry Coke and cherry lip balm were veritable pioneers of the fruit infiltration into hybrid profiteering, yet the unassuming cherry rarely makes a top ten appearance on a fruit consumer's desirability ranking. Number twenty-two on my list. Just how did the cherry manage to pop the confectionary drinks market? I do not know.

Because, for me, the very next fruit outside of the top four is the grape. The grape has been well diversified with the wine industry, and it was a masterstroke of grape marketing that has monopolized the medical care commerce. It baffles me still why more fruits have not managed to puncture the hospital visit dollar.

Why couldn't cherries crack the sick note? Cherries are essentially the same size product, as easily consumable, perfectly at home inside a small brown paper bag. There is no reason. Yet the cherry has constantly failed to be picked when such a consumable decision is offered.

Having said all that, my thinking is that the grapes have gone about it in the wrong way. The grape is targeting the queasy, with the selling point being that the grape is filled with goodness and might just help battle the plight of ill health. Well, the way I see it, there are many more people who are not sick than those who are sick. Prevention rather than cure. The grape should target the happy and the healthy. Have your relatives bring you grapes before you get to the hospital bed. That's the way I'd go with it. It's a much bigger market. And there's room for cherries.

So my advice to the public information advertisement people of New York, is don't waste your money reminding everyone about fruits because we know about them. Just make a handy little place where I can pinch an apple and shine it on my sleeve. Trade in a pizza vendor for a barrow boy; swap the coffee for a kumquat; cherish a cherry; let me grab at some grapes. A banana bonanza. Arrange a place where I can buy an orange. Orrange a place…. That doesn't really work, does it? Whatever.

The halftime oranges do their thing, and we stride off with the complete game spoils to win yet another tournament outing. It's just as well, as we require victories much in addition to performances for the recruitment drive. Travel soccer is taking a rather aggressive lemon twist, and this twist is starting to affect even the very youngest of players. My under ten girls turn full-sided select next year, and that means that we need about four or five quality recruits to come onboard and bolster the roster from the top. The main tactic is to play the elite tournaments and pick out and pick off the maverick players from the demolished opponent. Most of the time they come to you. Performance is everything, and the New York oranges redeem their search a justified one.

There is competition, mind you. No longer is the maverick American soccer parent content for their ten-year-old child to live out a fledgling soccer experience playing division one soccer in their hometown club with their hometown school friends. A new echelon of youth soccer is being created that will ensure that eleven-year-old players are conditioned to a regime of State Cup success. Division one with your mates is not good enough anymore. An eleven-year-old devotion to a mandatory training schedule is now governed by paternal influence. Success is paramount and failure unwelcome. But I don't even turn eleven until next

December. Fuck it; you will be driven forty-five minutes, three times a week to play at the highest State Cup standard. And there will also be a non-optional optional training session on Saturday mornings. But I kind of like playing with my friends. That's all gone now, sweetheart. You have a cup to win. But I don't even turn eleven until next December.

Recreation and enjoyment have been squeezed from youth development where laughter was once the only currency. It no longer works that way anymore.

I went select with my team to abandon the shackles of closed club hypocrisy. I went select to keep my team together. The new echelon of select will rip the very heart out of a number of different teams, including mine, and I can't help but feel that very little consideration has ever been given to the welfare of the players involved. When my players defect, or rather are made to defect, I will be left with half a team. It's not about players anymore, and I have to say that I don't much like it at all. I'm a very big one for elitism and pressure. I like the fact that my honeys are cognizant of defeat over victory, but Jesus fuck, guys, these kids are ten. Your kid is ten.

Super teams are now being formed ahead of select teams, and the migration is buoyant. Parents will push, pull, deceive, and then drive a player to the edge of happiness in the pursuit of involvement. I feel it important for a player to play at their standard, but I do also feel that there are boundaries that should not be crossed at such a tentative age. There are few who share my consideration, and the majority who don't share my consideration are the ones who actually have the final say. I'm just not sure that it's about players any more, but very much about parents, and that smarts a little.

Before the season is out, my top four players will be cherry-picked for the State Cup super team next year. And that's a banana skin that I just can't avoid.

#22: THE BROOKLYN BRIDGE

It has taken me nearly two years to find the time to honour the massive inclination of visiting my most anticipated New York City reverence. I couldn't really give a shit about the Empire State Building or any corroded green statues of liberation; I never really did much like the French anyway. And one sycophantic gesture doesn't seem to have been enough to win a contemporary American public or a burning Bush.

What I hold in the most regard as my pertinent city symbol is the Brooklyn Bridge. It took me twenty-six years to get to live in New York within touching distance of what I wanted and then another eighteen months to actually touch it. I guess that's just the demands of modern living city life.

My youth is riddled with the delusion of New York residency and was heavily punctuated with mob movies, Scorsese pictures, and classic sit-coms. None of these references had the Rockefeller Center or the Chrysler Building in their title track, but the vision of the Brooklyn Bridge artery delivering yellow cabs and gangsters to the shimmering city promise behind was pretty much the salient image that sold this town to me and above all other individual factors is the reason why I'm here.

To accentuate the value of visiting the bridge I took with me a tangible piece of my very own youth to share the pleasures and remember the reasons. I took with me my buddy and measure of all things good, who has recently begun his own New York chronicle. We walked long and fast and with great purpose, mocking street numbers all the way from Penn Station down Broadway and Lafayette and through Chinatown and the Lower East Side. We stopped only for coffee. Cigarettes were taken on the fly. We did rest at a park bench to adjust newly procured shoes, however. The task was far and arduous and could easily have been diluted with a ten spot taxi ride, but some why the achievement of reaching my bridge was made all the more worthy after actually achieving something. At the edge of Manhattan we started to see the congestion intensify as all roads lead over the East River. We walked tired and happy underneath the vast and high construction hitting the water bank directly below the dark and imposing stanchion. We marched the riverside trail, and as we moved north, the significance of my bridge came into glorious perspective.

We arrived at the transition of late afternoon into evening, and we stayed until nighttime. The string of fairy lights delicately picked the suspension cables, and all my movies and all my sit-com titles came back to me, sincerely holding a memory of why I wanted to be here. It's dark, it's black, and at the end of the day kid, it's just a bridge. But that was so not true for me. I looked far into the lights of the Brooklyn Heights, and it reminded me of Sydney's beautiful harbour. While Sydney's bridge-delivered North Shore is indeed a beautiful thing, Brooklyn appeared more urban and more sinister and way more interesting. I recall Sydney's North Shore appearing in very few of my mob movies.

The Manhattan piers shined incandescent with a funfair attitude to exterior lightbulb appendages and looked fantastic and welcome as the high-rise, money-making factories of Wall Street stood erect with arrogance behind. The picture was a postcard. But the scene is far from this fluffy. All the movies talked of how this location was an area of murderous retribution and felonious activity, traitorous minions dropped to the bottom of the East River after trying to skim a little off the top. Media reflects reality, correct? I mean, how contemporary and how appropriate is it that New York do-gooder Peter Parker and his spider-based pseudonym should find his evil octagon nemesis laired under the same incandescent funfair of the Lower East Side Piers and the South Street Seaport. And surely more gangsters inhabit the financial district than all the Italian enclaves in all of the five boroughs put together.

I have to say that it was no disappointment that we didn't interact with any crime or any criminals on our journey to my utopia. We sat between the Brooklyn Bridge and the Manhattan Bridge and smoked cigarettes, just looking at the achievement of engineering that has shaped a country, and just looking at the symbolism that has shaped a culture. Carefree joggers pounded the sidewalks, even under the cynicism of nightfall, and looked comfortable with the rhetoric that the bridge represents. Our shopping bag felt safe, even if the shoes inside were now old and redundant, having been upgraded immediately at the cash register. Oriental ethnics took leisure in angling from the riverbanks, pulling out five-eyed groupers from the mist for Canal Street sale. That's no way to earn a living.

I can safely say that the Brooklyn Bridge met my every expectation to a spectacular degree. I loved everything about it, and it was well worth my walk. I wasn't in the slightest bit disparaged to not meet a gangster digging a lime hole or even to have them replaced with athletes or the fishing Chinese. I still have my movies, and the bridge still commands the unsavoury representation of New York that I love. Well, to me it does anyway. The Brooklyn Bridge was no fugazy.

I live in New York, which is some three thousand miles away from my hometown. I chose to come here, but in choosing this I also chose to give up a few things, not least, my family. So what is my family now? Yes, the bridge visit might have been a feeble attempt to gain entry into the most known *family* in New York, but I am not a mobster. I do not have the requisite bloodline, and I did not meet my contact under the Brooklyn Bridge as anticipated. So I don't have *my* family, and I didn't get into *the* family, but I do have an alternative. I do have *a* family.

Tomorrow I return to being a soccer coach in New Jersey and my away day fixtures will see me travel south for a suburban rendezvous with my twelve little honeys. A twenty-five minute journey and an hour pre-game preparation should mean that a 2:30 PM kickoff warrants a 1:00 PM leave. I leave at 10:30 AM. Because I have my new family now.

While it would be just foolish to suggest that I have totally amicable relationships with all the families of the kids that I coach, I do have amicable relationships with some. Most family relationships progress no further than game-day acquaintances. I mean, who wants to socially converse with the guy who benches your nine-year-old child due to soccer ineptitude, or who wants to chat with the guy who writes a thousand word end-of-season evaluation highlighting fourteen areas of underachievement about your one and only little honey. Not many, that's for sure.

Not many, but not all.

My premature game-day departure takes me to the welcome and open arms of my new family. I arrive with hours in abundance and slip seamlessly into the family lifestyle that is not my family, but is the closest thing that I have to it. My reheated breakfast and sometimes not even tepid breakfast is slid at me on paper plates by my bathrobe-adorned surrogate mother as her never-to-be-seen-in-public bed hair represents my infiltration into the family circle. My nine-year-old sister and starting midfielder gathers cutlery, condiments, and syrup, while in exchange, I clean up her surface spilled apple juice. There is very much a Rudy and Theo thing going on that far transcends our soccer coach and star player association. My new middle sister asks me probing questions that I don't really want to answer, which is fine because she really doesn't care much about the replies given her preoccupation for hair grooming and social preparation.

I am not quite family, but then I am not quite a guest either. I fix my own coffee, now with the knowledge of where the sugar bowl is kept and the expectation that I utilize it unassisted, while the family bubbles along resolving the weekly conundrum of getting everybody ready for where they need to be. Drama, humour, and familiarity are so sincere, as the plight of the missing soccer cleat is performed in seven different rooms by four actors with varying degrees of interest—and played out with varying degrees of frustration and with the associated volume that correlates perfectly to that frustration. It could have been my home. What am I saying? It is my home.

I left Cardiff to come to New York, and I don't regret a single decision along the way. One of my most major influences was to try to embrace a little of the media reflection that has influenced so much of my adolescent growth and even my maturity. Seeing my bridge was a positive moment in the delivery of my New York experience, and more so than any other focal point so far, it reassured me that I had arrived in New York, and that made me happy and a little bit more fulfilled.

Even though I like to think of myself as an independent individual, I also think that I have made little secret about my fondness for my hometown and everything that it represents. When you leave your hometown, you leave many things; you leave your city, you leave your friends, and you leave your family. I think that I might have found a better city ... well ... for a while anyway. Friends come and go the older you get, the wiser you get, the richer you get, and the poorer you get. Family, however, is very different to leave or to change or to replace.

I may not have my family, but I'm kind of sharing someone else's family. And I very much like it.

#23: How Do You Keep Her?

My twelve little honeys just got the soccer club approval to go select for our U-11 season. Only now am I able to draft in some top-class out-of-towners during the transfer window, and only now can I finally cut "soap hands" the keeper. It's a good time to be a kid on my team.

Soccer clubs run their programs a little differently from each other. I spend most of my time working with a retroactive club of paralytic ambition. However, due to some combined forces of nature, my team is an anomaly team blessed with fine talent and an industrious work ethic to boot, which has caught the eye of the lethargy in command. Good for me and good for them. Unfortunately, what normally happens is these well-blessed players move on to less retroactive and less paralytic clubs. The reasons are obvious and yet never negated. My club wishes only in-town players to participate in the program, and so this delivers a vast range of ability on my roster between the State Cup quality stud player ranking number one by miles and "soap hands," the wheezing keeper propping up the team sheet with out-of-depth ineptitude. Rural Jersey commuter towns just do not have the population to raise a full-strength soccer team, and forbidding non-residential players in exchange for a hometown putz is a stubborn and detrimental standpoint. By the U-11 season, the top players have grown so frustrated with incompetent teammates that they inevitably wish for greater things and move up by moving on. The closed town soccer club regresses into a shambles of full-sided female soccer, while neighbouring towns flourish with your players.

It sounds a little contradictory, but the only way to keep in-town kids playing in town is to stop the crappy in-town kids from playing in town and bring in out-of-town kids from another town to now play in-town in your town. You need to get better players to join your team, which will satisfy the better players that you already have on your team, because now they have an appropriate place to play. You cut the bottom five in-town kids and replace them with five out-of-town kids so as you can keep ten in-town kids. If you keep the bottom five in-town kids in exchange for the five out-of-town kids, then your top five in-town-kids will go and play out-of-town instead. You need to make your program strong enough so that your players don't need to look elsewhere. And so the process begins with my team as we go select.

The recruitment and cutting process is severe, sinister, and underworld. While beautiful ignorance allows the ten-year-old girls to just play, the movements behind the scenes are often inappropriate when you consider that this is all done for the benefit of youth soccer. Maverick parents, ambitious coaches, and soccer clubs seeking rival team retribution work the number scams to try to recruit players. Legislation dictates that it is illegal to directly approach a carded player and attempt to tempt them to play for your team. Poaching is an act that will ruin a reputation within seconds if ever caught. The trick is to never get caught, and so the legislation just drives the enterprise underground. Surreptitious meetings, e-mail communications from non-traceable accounts, and after-hours phone calls fuel the comedy.

The recruitment process for my select team has begun, and five new stud players will need to be procured. I have my first meeting tonight—8:30 PM below the clock tower, have a copy of the *New York Times* under your left arm, and make sure that you're not followed. Ten-year-old girls, remember.

The cutting process is a difficult area to negotiate. From my current U-10 roster of twelve players, I am obliged to take nine in accordance with soccer club stipulation. Mind you, I do want to take nine. I think eight deserve a place, two have every chance of making it, and two should not really have been on the team in the first place. I want to take all twelve because I love them, but the truth is that only nine can really make it. Ten can make it if I fudge the figures, which I might have to do. Whichever way you look at it, eight, nine, or ten, someone has to get cut. I take the accolades of game-day victories and in equal dosage I have to take my medicine when it comes to dropping the goof-off kids and dropping "soapy."

The process is made even more difficult when the determined parents of the bottom four kids have vowed unwavering devotion to the project that is in total misalignment to their players' abilities. I know a good six months ahead of time that this little one just ain't gunna cut the honey mustard when it comes to choosing the select team "hot dogs." Dilemmas, dilemmas, dilemmas. However, six months is a long time in the propagation of ten-year-old girls. Things can change. My prescription is a course of intensive and expensive individual training that might just deliver a positive prognosis. A more menacing perception might read this as a situation engineered for personal profit, but I dismiss this as wrong. The creating of an environment of destined failure only to be redeemed by my personal tuition at sixty dollars an hour investment is indeed a very sound entrepreneurial adventure, but most definitely is not my entrepreneurial adventure. Hang on a minute though. That works quite well actually. Not my style, baby.

Religion pains me. Perhaps this is a little untrue; I don't think that religion is a pain to me until it is pushed. A bit like a bruise then. Okay, religion bruises me. The Great British Empire has allowed religion to slide away, and I'm happy with that. America, however, has not let religion get away so easily. And New York remains the salient example of my time. I have talked before about how New York has educated me much on the subjects of religion, and the more that I learn from this amazing city, the more that I find to write about. It still remains a little difficult for me to comprehend and understand just why so many New Yorkers muse to the religion thing, but then I guess that's up to me to work out rather than you. I confess though, I just don't get it.

When I am about my forever busy day, I always find a minute to take in a coffee. I feel that it's very important to do so. However, outside my chosen coffee vendor, I am endlessly embraced by two giant black mommas who occupy the front seats of a beat-up American car and try to punt out the word of God with some weak periodical. Communications discourse through a crack in the driver's side window as an attempt to divinely purify my failed existence is acted out. How dare a seventy-year-old woman with random companionship suggest that her inclination and a cheap-arse brochure be strong enough to deviate me away from my culture and into hers? It baffles me much how we ever got to the stage where God's disciples are passing the message around out of a '79 Cadillac's window. I can't imagine that this was in the quarterly merchandizing appraisal of the immaculate business model conceived upstairs by the big man. This is no immaculate concept. Fuck off and leave me alone. I'm not subscribing, and your attempts are pathetic.

It baffles me further why the black community of New York seems to hold so strongly to its religion. In the southern Bible Belt, you can kind of understand; having said all that it was not as if the good Lord had given the Southern black a nice bite at the cherry. Maybe a suck on the pip if you're lucky. Jesus is always portrayed as a Caucasian—Middle Eastern at best—so how the fuck has an African American community taken so strongly to such a hypothesis. Surely your historical grievance and contemporary chipped shoulders can't support such an endeavour. I find it embarrassing how the New York black comedian can trade off drive-by-shooting references and still find the association to slip in a gag about church shoes or observational rhetoric on Sunday school. It doesn't work for me. It's not that black comedy doesn't work for me; it's more that religion doesn't work for me, and the American Christian blacks are just one of many tribes consumed by the nonsense. I hate it.

The religion that bugs my world the most is the Jewish religion. More so than any other entity, the reason why my little honeys skip the most training sessions is Hebrew school. And it's Hebrew school that is starting to take a pinch out of the select team. The select team mandate clearly says that three ninety-minute training sessions will need to be adhered to for your selection to be considered. Failure to comply with this commitment level will result in failure to play. My first-choice keeper and genuine replacement for "soap hands," has a non-agreeable and non-negotiable commitment to religious study at a same time conflict as my mandatory Wednesday training session. So how do you keep her?

I can't live without her. Drastic times call for drastic measure.

While at a CVS pharmacy collecting a post-operative prescription for an ailing friend's knee ligaments, I purchased the answers to my prayers. Well … I purchased the answers to my keeper's prayers is what I actually did. For three dollars and ninety-nine cents I bought a book titled *365 Bedtime Bible Stories* by Barbour Publishing. Over one hundred illustrations, they'd have you know. The purpose for the read is not what you might think. I have not converted. I will never convert. I will *never* convert.

But I will study. And after study I can diversify my core competency. My keeper can't learn soccer education at Hebrew school, but now she can learn religious education at soccer school.

God told Moses to build a special tent to worship the Lord, and Moses was to protect the Ark of the Covenant inside the holiest of holies. In a similar and soccer way, you are Moses, and you need to stop the ball entering the tabernacle with your new Adidas goalie gloves. Some sharper footwork and better field positioning will help Moses here.

During Judges 7:16, Gideon divided his army into three parts to surprise the Midianites at the River Jordan. In a similar and soccer way, we too split our Israelites into three parts: a defence, a midfield, and an attack. We also like to surprise our opposition, not with cracked clay pot lanterns, but with counterattacking soccer. You will of course remember Cindy's winning goal in the Thanksgiving Day tournament against the Bloomfield U-10 Bombers; 4-3 to us in the final if anyone is interested.

You know how Ruth and Naomi were friends, and how Boaz looked after them and protected them. It's as if Ruth and Naomi were central midfield players and Boaz was a whole defensive unit that allowed the fullbacks to get forward in support as much as possible to create penetration down the flanks. That is exactly why God sent Boaz, and I think that you will agree that both Ruth and Naomi's goal scoring benefited as a consequence.

Rebecca and Abraham wouldn't have been caught offside like that.

Sixty dollars an hour for professional soccer tuition. Twenty-five dollars an hour for religious study. Special offer reduction of eighty dollars the pair.

Free to my select team keeper. Keep Her.

DRIVERS
ROAD TEST
ONLY
NO PRACTICE
DRIVING
KEEP OUT
#24
What's The Points in Arguing?

#24: What's the Points in Arguing?

All I ever see on New York billboards are adverts for car insurance. I suppose that with just so many cars on the road and without enough road to accommodate them all then any sort of coverage is big business. The counterfoil invoice from my bosses' insurance company has rocketed to astronomic proportions and now reformations are in place.

I am a courteous driver; I take it safe, and I take it easy on the road. Nothing to do with making our community an altruistic place to be that is; it has everything to do with ensuring that I stay alive and injury free until the end of the season. And so with the evident intrepidity of sharing a road with the buffoon New York driver, it is an act of necessity that I take it very safe. Unfortunately not all employees share this philosophy. When presented with someone else's go-kart the young male mind slips from any cerebral mounting that it might have once adhered to. With something like seventeen cars in the loop and with twenty-five or more drivers available to dilute the blame, the odd parking infraction or the occasional near-side abrasion seems irrelevant; irrelevant to those who might have to front for the damage, that is.

Midnight journeys back from the bar, unacceptable parking locations, and tricky little reversing manoeuvres are not even considered when you perceive that your car is made of rubber, and the tab gets sent to an invisible source. On day one induction to the company new guys are thrown a fifteen-minute appraisal of driving ability, and then they are thrown the keys. The streets of America are no longer safe. Bubblehead morons are driving on the wrong side of the road for the very first time, and most aren't at all sure that a left hand turn, once simple and quick given the British system, will contradict your passage in direct conflict with two lanes of fast-moving and unforgiving traffic. Chilling and true: idiots on the road, driving carelessly and recklessly with little concern for any other road users. And when you add in our bubbleheads to that cannonball concoction you have a veritable gumball rally on the avenues of New York and on the streets of Jersey.

Too many crashes and too many infractions to the company insurance claim have now raised this month's quote to disproportionate heights. One way to bring down the balance just a little is to ensure that all covered drivers have a New Jersey driver's license, where once it was not considered important as long as you had some sort of UK authorization. Another way to bring down the balance is to just stop crashing, but hey, I'm not in charge, and I don't make the rules. A driver's license doesn't make you less stupid; it just makes you permitted to remain stupid.

This has inconveniences for me. Throughout my time here I have mitigated to actually procure my N.J. driver's license, and now I have to do so on the authority of my paycheck-threatening boss. The deadline is one week. I have to scour the book and figure out how many feet away from a fire hydrant I can park on a Wednesday afternoon, and I have to trip the journey to the test centre to take the written exam. I designate forty-eight hours as revision time enough, and I glimpse the Web site for the information that I require.

Two days later I haven't flicked a page of the driving manual, and so I find myself trying to locate ID documentation enough to satisfy the six-point scheme enforced at the DMV front desk. I take the book to maybe get a few last seconds of revision during the inevitable queue that welcomes you at most institutional holdings like this. I park up at the gray building and slip through the '70s swing doors that require a little maintenance. The offices are ugly and crowded and not at all far from what I was expecting. Fat, black American women, disgruntled with their lack of college education, sit and scowl from the booths, while some degree of disorder unveils itself. Hispanic labourers struggle with the language, and the occasional high school girl accompanied by her father file up to be declined. There's an evident smell of urine coming from behind that pistachio door.

The unexpectedly amicable greeter asks after my visit and hands me the required documentation, which I fill out on the pistachio breakfast bar away from the mêlée. Some Mexican guys don't have a pen. I am unable to assist. I rejoin the line as is customary at this juncture and wait to be called forward.

So this black woman is about forty years old and must weigh about forty stone. She has terrible dress sense, and she doesn't want to be here. She asks for my ID documentation, and I begin to expose my life in an effort to accumulate the required six points and advance for testing. Passport, equipped with valid visa and current I-94. All good, two points. Now we're cooking. I even think that she's starting to warm to me. They all do in the end; it's fruitless to resist. Bank statement. One point. Okay, my bank statement isn't worth shit to anyone other than me, or the bank, yet my passport can get me into loads of countries. How is the passport only worth twice as much? What can a bank statement get you? I don't understand.

Paycheck counterfoil. One point. Still don't understand why a passport is only worth two.

"Social Security number."

"Yep, there it is on my paycheck."

"I need the Social Security card."

"I don't have the card. That's the number there on my paycheck that you just accredited with one point."

"But I need the card."

"I don't have the actual card, but the number is there on the paycheck that you just sanctioned as being legitimate."

"But I need the card."

"If I had the card, then it would show the same number as on the paycheck that you have already passed as being satisfactory."

"But I need the card."

"It's the same number on the card as on the paycheck."

"But I need the card."

"If you think that this isn't my Social Security number then you wouldn't have given me the point for the paycheck."

"But I need the card."

"Do you really need the same number on a different piece of paper?"

"Yes."

"I can write it on another piece of paper for you if that will help."

"But I need the card."

"How more legitimate is it if the number is written on another piece of paper?"

"But I need the card."

"The number isn't different on the card."

"But I need the card."

"The number is the same on the card as on the paycheck … and on this piece of paper that I'm writing it on."

"But I need the card."

"Do you think that this is my paycheck?"

"Yes."

"But the number on the paycheck is my Social Security number."

"But I need the card."

"Do you think that this number on my paycheck is my correct Social Security number?"

"Yes."

"Then do you really need the card to convince you I'm not lying?"

"Yes."

No point.

By now I'm really struggling. I'm rolling out all manner of shit. New Jersey Youth Soccer Association coach's pass. What? No point. But it has my photo on it, and state legislation allows me to work the sideline at a U-10 girls soccer game. Still no point. Blockbuster rental card? No point. She's not warming to me so much anymore. Bottle King loyalty promise? No point. But they've been trusting me for years. Titillations champagne room membership? Fuck off. Hang on, surely if I combine the Blockbuster and Bottle King together that's worth at least a point. Half a point? Security escorts me out. I don't scuffle.

That night I turn my belongings upside down and empty every drawer in the place. Finally, a moment of reprieve. I can shelve the champagne room membership hoax, as I have located my tangible Social Security card, and yes, it does have the same number on it as my paycheck—and on a small scrap of paper in my pocket. In the morning I try again.

Shit. It must be her day off. I have a new temptress to convince, though today I feel comfortable that I am indeed equipped with the necessary six points of identification. Passport, two points. Social Security *card*, two points. Blockbuster rental card … ah, just messing with you. I think she's warming to me. They all do in the end. Bank statement, one point. Paycheck counterfoi … "What's this?"

The visa has less than twelve months until expiry, and so I'm ineligible for the opportunity to apply for a driver's license. I can't sit the exam. I contest the arbitration and call for supervisory intervention. The intervening supervisor intervenes and vetoes my application. Security escorts me out. I don't scuffle.

Could this not have been made more prevalent at yesterday's debacle?

I find it odd how difficult it was to genuinely procure a genuine driver's license. It seemed that at every junction there was an obstacle put in the way to prevent me, and yet I had authentic integrity as my motive. Ironic that I was shepherded away from confirmation and told to rejoin the highway argument unqualified. Given license to drive home without a license at all.

978-0-595-43462-6
0-595-43462-2

the United States
'00003B/342/P

9 780595 434626